NEVER RUN AWAY

JULIE C. ROUND

OLDSTICK BOOKS

First published in 2014 by
Oldstick Books
18 Wiston Close
Worthing BN14 7PU

A CIP Catalogue of this book is available from
the British Library

Paperback ISBN: 978-0-9557242-4-4
Kindle ISBN: 978-0-9557242-5-1
epub ISBN: 978-0-9557242-6-8

Front cover image:
ID 8935463 © Artem Ilyushin | Dreamstime.com

Typeset in Adobe Garamond Pro 12pt by
www.chandlerbookdesign.co.uk

Printed in Great Britain by
Print-On-Demand Worldwide.

The publisher supports the Forest Stewardship Council® (FSC®), the leading
international forest-certification organisation. This book is made from
acid-free paper from an FSC®-certified provider. FSC is the only forest-
certification scheme supported by the leading environmental organisations,
including Greenpeace. Certificate: TT-COC-002641.

For Martin

One

Tony tried his wife's phone but could get no response. He felt like an idiot – worrying about a fifty year old woman, but she hadn't said she'd be late, had she? He couldn't remember. He just knew she was almost always indoors by five o'clock and starting tea.

They had a diary hanging up in the kitchen and he scanned it for appointments. There were none. Then he went to the larder and took out two slices of bread. If she wasn't going to get his meal on time he'd jolly well make himself a cheese sandwich. While he was at it he'd have a can of beer.

Taking his snack into the sitting room, he switched on the TV. It was all game shows and cookery programmes. He scrolled through the other stations but found nothing to hold his interest.

Picking up the paper he tried to read – snorting at the antics of some B-list celebrity. By half past five he was getting twitchy and by six o'clock decidedly worried.

He went into the hall and lifted the phone to check that it was still connected. He wouldn't have a mobile – didn't like to feel he was available at all times. The buzz on the land-line was temporarily reassuring. He tried to calm himself by watching the news – but by seven o'clock was beginning to feel ill. His mood vacillated between concern and anger. How dare she stay away and not tell him where she was? Had she had an accident? Could it be that she had deliberately left?

He marched upstairs to the bedroom and opened her wardrobe doors. All her clothes seemed to be there – but was there a small case missing? He tried to remember how many pairs of shoes she had but gave up. Frustrated, he ran back downstairs. Of course, her jacket was no longer on the hook in the hallway but that could just mean she was wearing it and maybe been delayed. In which case she would have contacted him, wouldn't she? She'd know he'd be worried.

Who could he ring? It was too soon to try the hospitals. He would ring their daughter. She might have a better idea of what had happened to her mother.

The phone rang and rang and he was just beginning to hope they were out somewhere together when Carole picked it up.

"Hallo, Carole Sharp,"she said.

"Carole– it's your father. Do you know where your mother is? She's not come home, or left a message."

"Gosh, Dad- it's gone seven o'clock. When did you last see her?"

Tony recoiled. He wanted answers, not questions.

"This morning – at breakfast. She didn't say she was

going anywhere special."

"What does she usually do on a Monday?"

Tony tried to remember. Did he know what Barbara did on a Monday? Did he know what she did on a Tuesday, Wednesday, Thursday or Friday? He couldn't answer that, yet he couldn't admit as much to his daughter.

"She usually goes into town to the market. She's usually back by four."

"Has she been feeling OK? Could she have had a doctor's appointment?"

"No. All appointments are written on the diary. She had her hair done last week and the dentist isn't for another four months."

"Then I'm sorry, Dad. I can't help – although you could check to see if her passport is missing."

Tony's heart gave a thump and he felt the blood rush to his head. The thought that his wife might have taken her passport led his fears along a completely new track. Had she been seeing someone behind his back? If so, it would have to have been in the daytime.

He dropped the phone and ran into the spare room. Opening the bureau he reached for the drawer which contained their passports. Yanking it open his hands closed on the small firm booklets. She had not run away. He let out a long breath that he hadn't realised he was holding and sat down abruptly on the spare bed.

He knew so little of her life outside the house. It hadn't seemed important. She didn't drive. She just shopped and cleaned and looked after the garden. Had she said she wanted new plants for the garden? Maybe the buses had changed their timetables? How long should he wait before alerting the authorities? What a right Charlie he would look if he did that and then she turned up safe and well and if she'd been involved in an accident surely someone would have contacted him by now?

Concern was giving way to rage. The thought that her absence might be deliberate seemed like a personal insult. Stupid bitch! How could she dare to go off and leave him with no note, no meal and the prospect of sleeping alone? That is, if he could sleep. He turned on the TV again and found a violent film that kept his attention for a while. Then he realised he was getting hungry. 'I'll show her,' he thought – and, grabbing his coat from the hook in the hall, slammed the door as he headed for the pub.

Next morning Tony woke early, dressed and made himself a cup of coffee -noticing, as he did so, that there was very little milk left in the fridge.

"You think I can't manage without you, Madam," he said to the empty house. "I'll show you."

He felt even more strongly than before that he couldn't risk the humiliation of going to the police. He would find her himself – and bring her back where she belonged.

What did he really know of her movements? One thing he was sure of- she had a part time job at the hairdressers in town, Cindy's Hair Salon, and she sat in when the other girls were at lunch on Tuesdays and Thursdays. She left him a salad on Tuesday and he went to the pub for lunch on Thursdays. Today was Tuesday. He'd go into town and see if she was there. If not, the other assistants would probably know where she was. Women always told each other their secrets, didn't they?

For a fleeting second he considered ringing the hospital but then decided to go there in person and pretend to be a visitor. If he asked after Mrs Sharp they'd be certain to tell him if she'd been brought in.

Once he'd decided on a plan of action he felt better. He was doing all a caring husband could do – wasn't he?

He rinsed the empy coffee cup under the cold tap and upturned it on the draining board.He didn't feel like making toast. He'd eat later.

It was a good thing he no longer had a job to go to. Being made redundant at 55 had been a great shock to him. He'd enjoyed being a coach driver – especially when he had a courier with him. But the firm had gone bust and no other company would take him. He would have to wait for his pension and, although the hours dragged, he'd begun to get used to being home all the time. He wished, sometimes that he knew more people in the locality but he'd joined the pub darts team and was a regular at the betting shop.

Barbara had always been the sociable one. He was aware that she went out to coffee mornings and did pilates once a week. That would be another line of enquiry.

He didn't take the car into town. They lived near enough for him to walk. At the hospital he made his enquiries but no-one answering Barbara's description had been admitted. He had a coffee and a doughnut in the hospital café and set off for the hair salon.

It was 12.15. If Barbara had been working she should be there.

First, he looked in through the window but no-one looked like his wife. Then, steeling himself against the overpowering smell of perm lotion and shampoo, he entered.

Immediately a tall blonde came over to him. "Can I help you?" she asked.

"Yes, I was looking for Barbara, my wife. She works here. I thought she'd be in today."

"Oh, I'm sorry. She said she was going away for a while. We're going to miss her."

So she had intended to leave and they would expect him to know all about it. He thought quickly. "I hoped I'd catch her before she went. I had something to give her."

"She wasn't in on Friday either. I suppose she was packing."

Friday? Tony shook his head. Had Barbara been working more days than he had supposed? He'd known she was earning some 'pin money' as he called it – but if she 'd been doing extra days...

"You'll be looking for someone to replace her then?"

"Well, we've got a new deputy manager but we will need a trainee."

"She didn't tell me she'd been made deputy manager."

"It was great having someone reliable. The young ones don't like doing full days."

Full days? What was she talking about? Did that mean his wife had been working full time on Tuesdays and Thursdays? And what about the other days? She'd always been at home at lunch time – but she'd been out most mornings and afternoons. He'd not bothered to ask where she was going.

He turned abruptly and left the shop, his fists clenched and his teeth grinding. She had deceived him – but for how long? His rage almost blinded him as his eyes searched for somewhere to vent his anger.

He was hungry again. He staggered into the nearest pub and ordered a pint. Then he looked at the menu. "I'd like an all-day breakfast," he growled.

"It will be about half an hour. Is that OK?"

He almost choked on his beer. "No , it bloody isn't!" He picked up his glass and slammed it down on the counter. "If you can't fry a few sausages and an egg in less than 30 minutes what kind of a place is this! He was spitting foam and the barmaid was cowering away from him. He turned left and right, searching for support, but the few customers were looking down, avoiding his gaze.

He took one long swig of his half empty glass and stormed out. Nothing was going right today.

He'd walk back past the fish and chip shop. Then he'd open another can of beer and have four slices of bread and butter. No-one would frown at him and sit across the table with a small plaice and half a dozen chips. He'd order mushy peas. That would be sure to make him feel better.

The one advantage of having the place to himself would be to avoid her unspoken criticism. If he wanted to pig out he would. His steps grew firmer . There was plenty of time to find the bitch. While she was away he would play – his way.

The next morning he was up early buying milk and bread from the corner shop. Then, fortified by a large bowl of cereal and two cups of coffee he returned to the bedroom and his wife's wardrobe. Barbara's clothes were hanging in one half of the cupboard but the other part consisted of a set of drawers.

He started at the lowest – which held socks,tights and belts, a woolly hat, an evening bag and three pairs of gloves. A long, slim box held a green and gold necklace that she rarely wore. When did they ever go anywhere where she needed to dress up? He must have given it to her years ago but he couldn't remember. He pushed the drawer shut and opened the one above.

This held nightdresses, petticoats, bra's and pants. Tony felt his pulse quicken and a lump came into his throat. He fumbled with the assorted underwear and closed the drawer with a shudder. A picture of the young Barbara, slim and eager, in a silky blue shift,came to him. She'd been so lovely then – lovely and willing. He shook his head to rid himself of the memory and pulled roughly at the next drawer.

It contained nothing but T-shirts, a couple of sweaters and a swimming costume. He pushed it shut and opened the top drawer. He'd expected make-up or jewellery but instead he found two shoe boxes, full of papers. Exultant, he took them out and placed them on the bed. If anything could tell him his wife's secrets it would be these. He didn't expect love-letters. He couldn't imagine her being unfaithful- but he hoped for some indication of the private income she had been amassing. Maybe there would be bank details? Maybe even a pin number? Maybe, too, there would be some clue as to where she'd gone.

The first box he opened was a disappointment. It was full of leaflets about places they had been when they were first married – holidays they'd been on with their daughter and photographs of Christmases long gone. They had stopped taking photos when Carole left home and now no longer even decorated the house for Christmas.

The last holiday they'd been on had not been a success. They had returned from Spain feeling worse than when they went away. They had nothing to say to each other and seemed to have run out of things that they had wanted to share. When was that? Six years ago? There were no more holidays once he'd been made redundant.

He turned to the second box. Underneath a dental appointment card and some shop receipts he found what he'd been looking for- bank statements. He was shocked to find they were in Barbara's maiden name – with her mother's address. But her mother had died a few months before and it had been Barbara's task to arrange for the house to be sold.

He hadn't been involved. He had been tired of people telling him about things that didn't concern him. At least she had stopped bothering him with gossip but it meant he'd lost track of what she'd been thinking.

He looked at the dates on the statements. They were old. The the last three months were missing. This confirmed what he was beginning to suspect.

His wife had been saving a considerable sum and could now have access to thousands of pounds!

He suddenly felt very cold. He would have to draw on his imagination – try to think how she would have thought – to find out what she had planned. He kept one sheet of paper and returned the rest to the box. He had his first clue. Next he would go to her pilates class and act the worried husband. He didn't care what the women there thought of him. He just needed to glean as much information about Barbara's mental state as he could.

After a supper of soup and toast he dressed in his track suit and trainers and set off for the leisure centre. Barbara's pilates class started at 7.30 but by 7pm he was at the door of the hall, waiting.

The first person to arrive was the class teacher and he began by suggesting that Barbara had missed the evening meal and he was worried that she'd not returned from a journey.

"Doesn't she have a mobile phone?" asked the teacher.

"No," he lied, with a sudden realisation that people can be tracked through their mobile phones, "not any longer," he added in case one of the others knew she'd used one.

"Sandra knows her best," said the teacher. "I'll introduce you when she gets here. She probably just got delayed."

"Did you expect her tonight?"

"Well, yes. She's paid up for the whole term, but when people are ill they don't always ring and tell me. There's Sandra, now."

Tony turned to see a slim dark-haired woman hurrying towards them. She was tiny, not much over five foot – but she had an air of brisk determination. Her brown eyes looked alert – as if she recognised Tony and knew why he was there.

"Hi Sandra," said his companion. "We need help. This is Barbara's husband. He was wondering if you knew where she was."

Tony thought he saw her back stiffen but her reply was unequivocal.

"No. I thought she'd get here before me. I hope nothing's happened to her."

Was that a challenge he detected in her voice? Women! Once they got together there's no knowing what they told each other about their lives – their PRIVATE lives!

Sandra had taken her phone out of her bag. "I'll ring her, shall I?" she said.

Tony nodded. Up until now he'd thought mobile phones unnecessary and intrusive but perhaps there were times when they could be useful – when you were trying to track somebody down, for instance.

"It's switched off. Perhaps she's somewhere she didn't want to be disturbed. Have you tried the doctor's?"

The conversation was heading in a direction Tony did not want to go.

"No, not yet. I'll see if she's at home and then I'll try the doctor's. Thanks for your help." He walked purposefully out of the hall.

Once outside he found himself shaking. He needed a drink- and time to decide the next course of action. He could do with help – but first he'd go home and search the places he hadn't looked. Barbara usually kept her phone in her coat pocket and there were at least five handbags of assorted colours which he hadn't opened.

One more day and he'd be forced to go to the police, otherwise it would seem as if he didn't care.

He almost walked past the supermarket and then realised he had to stock up with essentials. He was unused to shopping. Barbara usually did it alone. Even when they did a big shop he stayed in the car and listened to the radio.

He bought ready meals and frozen chips, a bottle of rum and some coke, a six pack of beer and a bag of jam doughnuts that were on special offer. He couldn't remember what else they needed. Next time he'd make a list. He was getting low on cash so he used the cash point and asked for a balance at the same time. His account looked intact. He'd been giving her £100 each week for housekeeping and nothing extra was missing.

Trudging home in the dark he felt irritated and gloomy. It was as if a black cloud had settled over him and nothing could lift it.

Suddenly he was knocked sideways by a moving object. It was a bicycle – being ridden on the pavement without lights. The rider was almost out of sight before he regained his balance.

"Watch what you're doing, you cretin!" he shouted after him. He'd kept hold of his purchases but his heart was beating fast and he had a pain in one ankle.

He limped to his front door and entered. Even the house seemed cold and unwelcoming. He'd have to check on the timing of the central heating. It was late, but there was something he had to do before he thought about going to bed.

Leaving the shopping in the kitchen he went into the bedroom and threw all the bags he could find onto the bed. Jackets and coats followed, until he had all the items he had to search in one place. He started with the coats – diving carefully into each pocket, throwing tissues onto the floor and putting receipts and loose change to one side. A half used tube of mints stuck to his hand and he had to lick his fingers.

The coats and jackets revealed nothing suspicious so, leaving them in a pile on the floor, he started on the bags. All the while he had a nagging feeling that he was missing something – that a bag he knew he had seen was absent. Which one was it ? Could he remember the size, the colour? Reaching inside a white shoulder bag he felt something cold and hard. He pulled it out. It was Barbara's mobile phone. She had gone out without it – something she never did.

He felt a jolt of exultation. This would give him some clues. He tried to turn it on but it was completely dead. She had left nothing that would help him find her. He threw the phone across the room. Lipsticks and a comb followed. He began to tip the contents of the other bags onto the bed. There wasn't much. A library card – a few advertising leaflets and finally, a credit card. She'd gone away without her credit card!

He knew then – she had to be using a different name. For months, perhaps even years, she'd been planning this – saving her earnings so she could leave him. Why hadn't he seen this coming? She'd gone on cooking for him, doing his washing, even seeing to his needs in bed, although they weren't as frequent as they used to be. He got more pleasure looking at the girls on the porn sites. After all, how could a fifty year old with a thickening waist and greying hair compare with what was on offer on the internet?

He was tempted to turn on the TV but he knew if he did he'd be watching most of the night.

Instead, he made a list of all the people who might have known his wife's plans.

Who could he bring himself to talk to about his predicament? He would have to confide in someone and reluctantly he felt it should be their doctor. After all – doctors had to keep their patients' confidences didn't they? If the doctor thought he should go to the police he would do so.

Once the decision was made he felt more at ease. He cleared up the bedroom and, as he did so, realised what was missing. There was a space where the weekend case on wheels had stood in the base of the wardrobe. His senses sharpened. He looked for the full length belted macintosh that his wife sometimes wore over her jacket. That, too, was missing. He was beginning to build up a picture of how she would look.

He checked her shoes. Sure enough, her long boots were no longer there – and she thought she could get away from him! He smiled to himself. There were CCTV cameras at the station, weren't there? If she'd left the district by public transport he'd soon find her. If she'd gone anywhere it would probably be London. How could he get to see if she 'd taken a train? He returned to the first box and retrieved two photographs of his wife.

Tomorrow he would start to track her down.

Two

It wasn't until the train pulled out of the station that Barbara felt herself relax and the stiffness in her neck ease. She pulled the wheeled case into the space under the table and hugged the bulky holdall to her.

She'd done it! At last she had escaped. After all the months and years of planning she could hardly believe the moment had come when she'd actually left her husband and was on the way to a new life.

Was it too late? she wondered. Yet it was only recently that she had felt brave and disciplined enough to execute what she hoped would be a complete disappearance.

So much had bound them together in the early days of their marriage when they seemed so well suited. Then they had shared new experiences and were both overjoyed when their daughter arrived. Barbara had slipped easily into the maternal role. She was happy to stay at home while Tony became one of the coach company's most trusted drivers.

She relished the time spent listening to stories of all the places he had travelled and, once a year, she joined one of his trips. Her mother had looked after Carole while they travelled all over Europe, sunbathing by the Mediterranean and exploring French, German and Dutch cities and countryside.

Then Carole left home for college and Tony began to stay away longer. She returned to her old job as a hairdresser, hiring a chair in a shop in town, but spending more and more time with her elderly mother. As she often slept at her mother's house it did not seem peculiar to continue using her maiden name for work and have her business post sent to that address.

It wasn't until Tony was made redundant, however, that she began to see her savings as an escape route. Her husband had changed out of all recognition. He seemed to have retreated into a brittle shell. He had no interest in anything but himself and showed no imagination in searching for something to occupy him. If she offered a suggestion it seemed to infuriate him and he would storm off to the betting shop and stay away until the next meal time. She could no longer discuss or choose television programmes that might suit them both. She felt like a piece of furniture – a part of his life only because she was familiar – tolerated rather than loved.

She thought of the last time she had hidden in the kitchen so that he did not see her tears. All she had done was breeze in cheerfully with a pot of jam a neighbour had made, but he was engrossed in the paper and shouted at her for disturbing him.

"You know what I think of that old gossip," he had

declared. "I can't think why you encourage her."

Her good mood was shattered and, seeing the unreasonable rage on his face, she had felt herself begin to weep.

The thought that this might continue for the rest of her life was unbearable and it was her husband's negative attitude and lack of interest in how she spent her time that had enabled her to plan her escape.

Barbara made her way to the toilet and tucked the beret she had been wearing into her handbag. She tried on the auburn wig she had bought specially as a disguise. Her optician had supplied her with some polychromatic varifocals which were completely different from the reading glasses she sometimes wore and, removing her mac, she surveyed the woman in the smart navy suit in the mirror with satisfaction. The train juddered over some points and she quickly unlocked the toilet door and returned to her seat. The carriage was only half full and she didn't think anyone had noticed her transformation. She would have to discard the mac soon, it was too heavy to carry with her.

She wondered how Tony had reacted when he found her gone. She guessed he would ring their daughter but Carole knew nothing of her mother's plans. In fact, she had confided in no-one. Tony had known she had a separate account but he'd believed it was only from a few hours work each week and thought she spent it on luxuries and presents. Instead, she had risen to assistant manager in the shop and had been hoarding her salary until she felt she had enough to leave him. It wasn't difficult to buy a sovereign each month from her wages. She just didn't know how much she would need to be able to get herself settled somewhere else.

She had decided to keep her old bank account but only use it to put any followers off the scent. It would be there for an emergency.

All her spare time had been filled with plans for her escape and she could hardly believe that she had managed to keep Tony from recognising that something had changed.

The death of her mother had been the catalyst. After she had given Carole her share and paid off their mortgage she still had a substantial sum but, surprisingly, Tony had shown no interest in how much. He was angry and hurt that she had been the one to make them financially stable and she didn't expect him to show gratitude. She had made one last effort to elicit some kind of connection with him, trying to find something that would make him feel life together was worthwhile, but when she suggested a cruise he'd sneered at her and said all people ever did on board ship was eat and didn't she think she was fat enough already.

Arriving at Victoria, she booked into a small hotel under her maiden name. If Tony traced her to London he would have to be quick. She was only staying long enough to get another new image, with new clothes, new luggage and a whole new identity. Once she was unrecognisable she would leave London and move somewhere he could never find her. She felt uncomfortable wearing a money belt but didn't want to leave all her cash in the room.

She wanted to buy a new bag to take the place of the

ugly holdall she had brought with her. Her case held few clothes. She intended to buy different underwear from the white bra and pants she had been wearing. Her new personality would wear black or flesh coloured lingerie and silky pyjamas instead of her old cotton nightdresses.

The shops were as crowded as she had hoped and she soon had everything she needed to change her image. 'I must try to walk differently,' she thought and began walking with shorter strides as she tried out her new shoes in the hotel bedroom.

Her next task was to change her hair. The red wig was discarded. She would get rid of it later. She took her purchases into the en-suite bathroom. With a towel round her neck she studied the instructions on the packet. It was really simple for someone with her experience. It wasn't quite so easy to cut her own hair but she was determined to be drastic. She took out a pair of hairdressing scissors and hacked at her long brown hair until she had a short crop.'I look like an ageing Audrey Hepburn' she thought.

Next, she opened the box of bleach and put on the plastic gloves enclosed. Light Ash Blonde was the colour she had chosen and within an hour she was towelling her new , short style. She would need the red wig to leave the hotel but for the next stage of her plan she would be a blonde.

Next morning Barbara left the hotel – took her macintosh to a charity shop, used her cash card, possibly for the last time, at a nearby bank and then, dressed in a cream trouser suit with a paisley scarf over her newly trimmed hair, made her way to Victoria station.

She had practised her new name, Tania Baker, until it seemed natural and had chosen not to try to hide away in a remote region, like Wales, which had been her first thought. No- if she moved too far away she would stand out as a stranger. She'd head for the south coast, somewhere Tony had refused to consider as the beaches were too stony and the hotels too expensive. She wouldn't go to a hotel, she'd find a little B and B and look round for some kind of live-in occupation where they would not ask too many questions.

The train sped past rows of terraced houses, their long gardens bordering the line, until low factories and cluttered yards gave way to green fields and trees.

Barbara tried to relax. 'I am no longer Barbara Sharp' she told herself, 'I am Tania Baker.' She removed her scarf and looked at her reflection in the window. Had she really escaped? Was it possible in this day and age to adopt a completely new identity? She would have no records, no birth certificate, no passport, no national insurance number. She would have to do without a pension. She would need to stay fit for as long as possible. It would take time to become absorbed into a different society but as long as Tony could not trace her she would be content.

She closed her eyes for a moment and felt the tension drain from her shoulders. It almost felt like a holiday.

She woke with a start to find that hers was the next stop. She manoeuvred her two matching cases to the doorway and stepped carefully down onto the platform. She still wasn't comfortable in heels, even if they were only two inches high.

She had to suppress a delighted giggle. She felt so different, so light, so adventurous. It really was like being reborn.

She didn't walk far. She knew the lodgings near the beach would be the expensive ones – but she found a little terraced house with a 'vacancies' sign in the window and pushed the bell. The house was called 'Downsview,' although Tania (as she would now think of herself) could not see the Downs.

The lady who answered the door was enveloped in a floral overall and there was a warm cooking smell wafting from the back of the house.

"You have vacancies?" Tania asked.

"Yes, my dear – but do come out of the draught. I'm in the middle of baking. If you follow me I'll see to you in a moment."

Tania obediently trotted behind her into the kitchen.

"There's two rooms vacant on the first floor. I'll just get these out of the oven and take you up. Are you on holiday?" Not waiting for a reply she opened the oven door and took out two trays of scones.

"They smell delicious." remarked Tania.

"Yes, I do like cooking but most of our guests eat out. Now, leave your cases under the stairs and I'll show you the rooms."

"I'm not sure how long I'll be here," Tania began, nervously.

"Well, see if you like the room and we can take it a week at a time. I don't let for less than a week."

"That won't be a problem."

"Of course evening meals and snacks are extra. We

don't have a bar."

She ushered Tania into a small room with flowered wallpaper and white voile curtains.

"There's also a blind, but we aren't overlooked here at the back."

Tania went over to the window and was immediately glad she hadn't ventured far from the station. Over the surrounding rooftops and in the distance she could see the smooth green curve of the South Downs.

"Downsview," she smiled.

"Yes, but only at the rear, I'm afraid. There is a sink but the bathroom is shared with the other room on this floor."

The next room was larger, painted pale green with a double bed and fitted cupboards.

"This room has its own toilet. It is thirty two pounds a night, with breakfast. The smaller room is thirty pounds. The top floor is occupied by a writer and we live on the ground floor."

Tania wished her companion would stop talking. "Thank you, Mrs...?"

"Lane – Mrs Lane, but you can call me Gloria. Well, would either room suit you? I'd need a deposit."

"This room would be lovely. I can pay you for a week in advance if that would be acceptable."

"My dear, how wonderful. Do come downstairs and sign in. What do I call you? We could have a cup of tea and a scone."

Tania laughed. "That's very kind. I'm sure I'm going to like it here."

She'd have an address. Gradually she would become part of this place. She felt excited. She'd chosen the larger room because it was at the front. She wanted to be able to see who came to the house. She could hardly believe that she had gained her freedom. For a while she'd be looking over her shoulder but, for now, she felt proud of herself and optimistic about the future.

Next morning Tania left the house determined to explore her new district. First, she headed for the sea, revelling in the fresh, salty air as she strolled along the promenade.

It was cool, and the foam-tipped waves brushed greedily at the shingle. She would need gloves as the weather cooled, she thought, and turned towards the shopping centre.

She couldn't help looking out for the hairdressing salons. She counted four before she went into a department store for a coffee. Sitting at the window, she tried to plan her next move. She would need a local newspaper – and she had to establish a routine. She couldn't spend all her time wandering the streets.

She had seen a sign for a hospital. That might be somewhere she could investigate, and there was an information centre and a public library.

Her first task would be to remain patient. She had to become part of the community without drawing too much attention to herself.

The assistant in the shop offered her a store-card when she bought a pair of navy gloves but she declined. 'One day,' she thought, 'I'll say yes.'

The hospital was a pleasant surprise. It felt warm and light and had a brand new wing which held a large café.

The meals were cheap and the place was filled with nurses and visitors. Tania decided this would be her lunch stop. It was early, but her feet were tired. She'd spent the morning walking and wished she hadn't abandoned all her flat shoes. How could she keep her elegant persona and yet stay comfortable? Maybe she should copy the queen. She seemed to wear court shoes with a medium heel, when she wasn't in Wellington boots!

"Do you mind if I share your table?" A voice interrupted her thoughts.

"No – do sit down. I was daydreaming."

"Thank-you. It always fills up in here after twelve o'clock."

The stranger put her tray down on the table and settled herself in the seat opposite Tania.

"Are you visiting someone?" Tania asked, not wishing to seem impolite.

"Yes, my father. He's had a bit of a scare, but he's getting over it."

She broke a piece off her seeded roll and dipped it into a bowl of soup. "How's the salad?"

"Oh, fine." answered Tania, trying to guess the age of her companion. She reminded her a little of Carole, although her daughter was tall and dark whereas this girl had mousy hair, tied in a ponytail.

Thinking of Carole made her uncomfortable. She would have to explain her actions to her daughter but not until she felt confident about what she had done.

"Are you here to see someone?" the young woman enquired.

Tania paused before answering. What cover story

could she have for being here? She must stay as near the truth as possible.

"I'm thinking of going back to work," she said, "but I'm not sure what."

"What did you used to do?"

"Shop work," Tania replied. She wasn't going to say hairdressing. That would be too much of a give-away.

"You'll have problems there, then. All the shops are closing – except the charity shops. If you started as a volunteer perhaps you could become a manager."

"That's a really good idea," Tania smiled. "You've been very helpful. I hope your father is better soon." She drained her cup of tea and rose to leave.

"Thank you," the girl responded.

'Perhaps volunteering in a charity shop would be a good first step,' thought Tania and she vowed to look out for them as she made her way to the library.

However, once inside, she felt too tired to continue her enquiries. She sat day dreaming with the local paper open on the table in front of her. 'I must think what to do about the evening meals,' she told herself. She was sorry she hadn't mentioned the subject to Gloria at breakfast. She didn't feel hungry now – but she didn't fancy going to a restaurant on her own. 'I'll get some cheese and crackers – and a bottle of wine,' she thought, 'and I'll ask about dinner tomorrow.'

She wanted to return to her room but first she'd try her luck at a charity shop, buy a couple of novels and get a feel for the place.

The shop had a good window display and was light and airy inside. The clothes and bric-a -brac were at the front and the rear of the shop was lined with books.

Tania chose two novels and took them to the counter, a display cabinet full of jewellery.

An elderly lady in a turquoise twin set took the books. "That will be one pound, please."

Tania handed her the money, but before she could ask about a position the assistant said, "Could I interest you in our Christmas cards?"

'Christmas!' thought Tania. 'In October!'

"Perhaps another time." She suddenly felt too shy to ask about volunteering. Maybe the shop was too exposed. Maybe she should give herself more time. She hurried out, found a mini-market for the rest of her purchases and trailed home – feeling mentally and physically exhausted.

Three

Tony wouldn't ring the surgery to make an appointment. He didn't know how to explain what he needed over the phone. It wasn't far. He walked in, ignoring the hand gel on the wall, and stood behind the woman talking to the receptionist.

When his turn came he tried not to sound too abrupt.

"I need to see the doctor urgently about a personal matter," he began. "I think someone is in danger."

"And your name is?"

"Tony Sharp – 27 Green Street."

"Who is your doctor, Mr Sharp?"

"Dr Burton – it won't take long. I only want to ask one question."

"I'll see if she can fit you in between patients. Would you wait in the waiting room, please?"

It was twenty minutes before his name was called and the doctor did not look pleased to see him.

"Now, what's the trouble, Mr Sharp?"

"It's Barbara. I need to know if she was seeing you about anything. She's gone missing and I don't know where to turn."

"How long has she been missing?"

"Since Monday. It doesn't seem long but it is very unlike her. Can you help?"

"I'm afraid I can't. Barbara hasn't been to see me for months." She turned to her computer screen. "There's nothing to suggest she had any physical problems. I think you'll have to go to the police, or the Salvation Army. They find missing people."

Tony looked at her calm face with her neat hair and her crisp pink blouse and felt the urge to grab her by the shoulders and shake her. His hands clenched by his sides.

"I must see the next patient now, Mr Sharp," she said, more gently – as if she could sense his distress.

"I know. Thanks for your time," he managed to splutter as he almost staggered out of the room.

He didn't like the idea of visiting the police station but it seemed as though that was what he would have to do. Every time he thought about how his wife had left him he found it difficult to concentrate. He needed to be focussed and reasonable but he felt full of a kind of boiling, purple rage. He didn't dare go for a drink. It wouldn't do to breathe alcohol all over a member of the police force.

He felt for the photographs in his pocket. Maybe they would allow for the fact that he was upset. That was it! He'd play the desperate husband concerned for his wife's safety.

He stumbled into the police station and saw immediately that there was a civilian behind the glass partition.

Not only that – it was another woman! No wonder there were no jobs for men. They were all taken by females. He felt the bile rise in his throat and swallowed quickly.

"I need to see a copper," he demanded.

"Is there anything I can help you with?" she responded.

"No. It's about something personal. I think it may be a criminal matter." That should get her out of her chair!

"I'll ring through and see if anyone is available. Can I have your name, please?"

"Tony Sharp. It's urgent."

"Right, Mr Sharp."

A few minutes later a lock buzzed and a uniformed policeman put his head round the door. "Mr Sharp?" he said.

"Yeah, that's me."

"I understand there is some kind of crisis. Would you come through?"

"Thanks." He followed the constable into a tiny office.

"What can we do for you, Mr Sharp?"

"It's my wife. She's missing."

"The desk clerk could have dealt with that. How long has she been missing?"

"Since Monday."

"Three days. Do you have any reason to suspect she is in danger?"

"I don't think she's in her right mind. I think she may have taken a train to London. Can you check the CCTV at the station for me?"

"Could she have gone with someone else, or is there anyone she might be visiting?"

"No." Tony was getting frustrated. They weren't going

to take this seriously and he wanted to get on her trail as soon as possible. "I've got a photograph."

"Good. Have you any idea what she was wearing?" The policeman began to take notes.

"Yes – a cream trench coat and long black boots. She may be using the name Barbara Hastings. She had a brown case on wheels. Please, it's so unlike her."

"Mr Sharp, I must ask – have you had a falling out recently?"

"No. I love my wife and I just want her back." Was that convincing enough? he wondered.

"Well, I'll see what we can do. If the BTP find someone answering your wife's description I'll let you know. Meanwhile we'll circulate other forces but be aware, if an adult wants to disappear we can't stop them."

It wasn't satisfactory, but it was a start.

He'd hire some DVDs and get a curry. He'd have a real man's night in.

Tania decided to have a nice relaxing bath. She knew no-one else lived on the same floor so she could choose her own time, but she checked with Gloria, anyway.

"That's fine, lovely," said her landlady. "There's plenty of hot water. Have you got enough towels?"

"Oh dear, that's something I haven't bought yet."

"Never you mind. We have plenty. I'll bring you a couple to use for now."

She bustled off and came back with two fluffy white towels. They were warm and Tania held them up to her face.

"They've just come out of the airing cupboard,"

explained her landlady. "If there's anything else you need, just ask."

"I would like to have my evening meal here tomorrow, if that's all right."

"Good – just tell me the day before and you can eat here whenever you like. I'm afraid I don't do Sunday lunch. That's the family day."

"Thank you. I mustn't keep you." She had the feeling Gloria wanted to go on chatting but she was too tired to be sociable.

She would have to get undressed in the bathroom. Her bathrobe was hardly suitable for wearing in the corridor but she had left her thick practical one at home. She also had no bath essence but there was some liquid soap on the basin and as she lay soaking in the steaming bath she felt utterly relaxed.

'I'll have my nails done,' she thought. 'I've never had a manicure – and I'll find an exercise class. I could do with losing a bit of weight.'

Once dry, she tucked her clothes under her arm and returned to her room. She would sample her cheese and crackers, have a glass (or tooth mug) of the wine she had bought and tuck herself up in bed with a book. Tomorrow she would find a street map and explore. She was determined to become part of this community as soon as possible.

With a room above the front door she could hear each time someone entered or exited but, usually, nothing else. This evening she thought she heard footsteps climbing the stairs. They were slow, steady steps. It wasn't Gloria.

They seemed to pause outside her door and she could hear the laboured breathing of someone who found climbing stairs an effort. She couldn't help her muscles tensing and she waited – wondering what would happen next – willing the stranger to go away.

Eventually she heard a sort of shuffle and the footsteps continued, a creak from the stairs showing they were carrying on upwards.

Silly me – it must be the writer, thought Tania as she let out her breath in relief. But her peace had been shattered. She got out of bed and looked for a hiding place for her money belt. She didn't want to take the ten sovereigns it contained with her everywhere she went. She opened the wardrobe door and stuffed the belt into one of the long boots she had brought with her – the only item of clothing she could not bear to part with. They had cost her £100 and she wanted to keep them for the winter. After all, there were plenty of people who wore black boots, weren't there? She wasn't going to part with her favourite footwear just because Tony knew she had them.

The thought of her husband made her shiver. What was he doing now? she wondered. Had he discovered that she had gone to London? She hoped so – and that knowing where she might be had made him realise that searching for her would be like looking for a needle in a haystack.

Next morning Tania wandered through some of the side streets towards the town centre.

Coming across a jewellers, she stopped to read an

advertisement in the window offering to buy gold. Then her eyes were taken by the display of earrings and she had a sudden desire to get her ears pierced. Tony had always stopped her, before, but now she entered the Aladdin's cave of sparkling jewels and clocks and stood, admiring a beautiful pair of earrings like tiny stars hanging from a golden stud.

"Can I help you?" asked the assistant.

"Yes, please. I really need some advice. I'd like a set of earrings but I need to get my ears pierced first. Do you know where I could get that done?"

"Certainly. You won't have to go far. The hairdressers on the next corner will do that for you. You do know you have to have pure gold studs in first, until the hole heals?"

"Yes, thank you. I'll be back."

"Would you like us to hold onto the earrings for you? If you show me which ones they are we can do that."

"Thank you. I hope to be back by the end of the month."

Tania felt energised by her decision and when she saw the hairdressing salon she felt a stirring of familiarity. Stepping inside, it felt like a homecoming. The décor was modern, with grey and silver fittings on a lemon yellow wall. The girls wore light grey overalls with yellow piping and they all looked as if they cared about their own appearance.

The salon was busy – all four chairs were occupied, with another customer under the drier and someone having their hair washed at the sinks in the back room.

If she was still Barbara she would have asked if they could take her on, but no – it would be too easy for someone to track her down if she went on working in her old field.

A tall redhead was leafing through an appointment book at the desk.

"Excuse me. I believe you do ear piercings?" Tania enquired.

"Yes, but Jenny is only here Mondays and Tuesdays. Would you like me to book you in?"

"Yes, please."

"I have to ask – have you any medical conditions that might be a problem?"

"What! Oh, no. I'm perfectly fit." Tania felt herself blushing. If they asked who her doctor was she couldn't say.

"How about 10.30 on Monday. Would that suit you?"

"Sure." Tania felt at ease and knew that even if she didn't find employment here she would probably become a customer.

Happier, now she decided to return to the hospital for her lunch. Gloria had not told her what was for dinner. She hadn't asked so she would try to choose something unlikely. When she reached the restaurant she found vegetable curry on the menu so she ordered it, with a roll and butter and a cup of tea.

She had hardly got seated when she was joined by her companion from the previous day. "Hallo, there. I didn't introduce myself yesterday. I'm Fiona – is this place free?"

"Of course. It's nice to see a friendly face. Tania, Tania Baker. I do hope you don't mind the smell of curry."

"That's OK. I think you'll find it isn't very hot. It's what I call an English Curry."

"How's your father?"

"Getting better – but they say he'll have to stay in for another week for tests."

"Do you live with him?"

"Yes – me and Monty – that's the dog. We aren't far away – in one of those monstrosities across the park behind the hospital."

"I haven't been round there." Tania buttered her roll and watched while Fiona unwrapped her sandwich. "No soup today?"

"No. I don't like tomato."

"Do you work nearby?"

"Yes. I'm in the office at the Housing Association."

"That must be interesting."

"Not really. I handle complaints and repairs. It's a bit thankless."

Tania ate thoughtfully. Fiona might be a useful contact once she'd established herself in the community. "I hope we meet up again," she said, as her new friend rose to leave.

"I'll be back tomorrow," she replied, cheerfully.

With nothing to do after lunch Tania strolled through the park to the road beyond. The houses were large three storey, terraced, Victorian, she supposed.

As she studied them a short, squat woman rushed out of a front door, slamming it behind her, and ran down the path, pulling open the gate just as Tania was going past.

"Bossy old cow," she muttered as she swerved to avoid Tania. Then she paused. "I hope you're not going in there," she growled. "I pity anyone who has to deal with that old snob."

"Why? What's the matter?" Tania felt obliged to respond.

"She is – she says she wants a companion but what she really wants is a slave. I deserve some time of my own, don't I?"

"Are you from an agency?"

"Yes, but this was her last chance. She's had three 'companions' from us and she just doesn't know how to treat people. I'm going back now to report but the boss said if she didn't keep me he'd not send anyone else. He's washing his hands of her."

"Can I come with you? I'm looking for work."

"Fine, get in." She opened the passenger door of a light blue hatchback and Tania got in. Yet somehow she felt uncomfortable in the care worker's car. This wasn't what she should be doing. She was getting caught up in the official world of work – something she dared not do. Even when Pauline introduced herself and tried to engage her in conversation she felt that something was wrong.

The feeling of gloom deepened when she met the manager. A stout, florid, man with a tiny moustache, he seemed fussy and wouldn't look her in the eye.

"Pauline tells me you would like to work for us. Is that correct?"

"I'm looking for work. I thought you might be able to help."

"Have you done this sort of work before?"

"Only with my mother. She was ill for some time and I cared for her."

"So you can't supply references?"

"No – I used to work in a shop."

"Well, if you've had no training we can't take you without references. Our clients need to know they are getting qualified staff. Have you considered cleaning?"

He leaned back in his chair with a smirk.

Tania felt a blush creeping over her face. The man was a bully in disguise. She'd foolishly got herself into an awkward situation, just because she had felt that destiny had led her to that house. Now she had to get out as quickly as possible.

"I'm sorry I've wasted your time. It was Pauline I was trying to help. Thank you for seeing me." She lifted her chin and made to leave.

"I think your age may be against you," he retorted, spitefully.

She left, angry, and stood, shaking, on the pavement, trying to get her emotions under control. Her new persona was proving a façade. She couldn't help reacting as Barbara would to a man who was belittling her. Once again she wanted to run away but, instead, she found a tiny café tucked behind a church and ordered a pot of tea and a toasted teacake.

Calmer, she realised there was one way to gain victory over the situation. She would go back to the house and volunteer her services to the person who lived there. If she could care for her mother for years, and put up with her husband for even more, she must have the strength to cope with anything the old lady could offer.

Once she had made the decision it was easy to march round to the street, mount the steps, and ring the bell.

At first she thought no-one had heard and was about to ring again when the sound of bolts being drawn preceded the opening of the door.

Standing inside was a tall, thin lady, her grey jersey dress clinging to her gaunt frame like dust sheets over furniture. There were dark shadows round her sunken eyes and her cheekbones stood out like the bones of a skull.

"Yes?" she enquired, in an imperious tone.

"I understand there is a vacant position," responded Tania, straightening her back, determined not to be intimidated.

A flicker of amusement crossed the other's features. "How did you know that?"

"I met your last carer."

"Not carer, companion – but she was hardly that. Come in." She led the way down a dark corridor and into a high ceilinged lounge.

Tania looked round. The place looked like a museum. All the furniture was large and dark, the carpet worn and two walls covered with paintings. By the bay window stood a piano and behind the door there was a complete wall of books. There was no sign of a television or anything modern.

"Sit down," the lady commanded, "and tell me why you are here."

She doesn't need a carer, thought Tania. I really shouldn't be doing this. But something about the woman made her want to tell the truth.

"I'm new to the area and I have to find a job. I have left my husband and I don't want him to find me. I have had experience looking after my mother and when I met your last companion it felt as if fate had led me here."

"Did she tell you why she didn't stay?"

"No – but she did say the agency wasn't going to send anyone else."

The lady smiled. "What do they call you?" she said.

"I'm Tania, Tania Baker. I'm fifty years old, quite fit, and I can cook and do most household chores."

"Where are you staying?"

"I'm at Downsview, a B and B."

"But you can't stay there for ever?"

"That's true – but I've not been there very long."

"If I were to offer you £500 a week to live in – would you take it?"

Tania was astounded. She hadn't expected that. "What would I have to do?"

"Nothing you wouldn't do in your own home; cooking, cleaning, shopping – but most of all you would have to entertain me."

"Entertain?"

"Nothing sordid, I assure you – but I get terribly bored. I don't need the kind of care that people from the agency are used to providing. I need company and that is what they were not able to give."

"I think I could do that."

"How about a month's trial? You could have the whole top floor."

"You'd trust me? Without references?" She was beginning to feel rushed into something she hadn't bargained for.

"Poppycock! The others came with references and look what happened. No – I think you have more spunk. I'll expect you on the first of next month."

Tania realised she had been dismissed and meekly followed her companion to the front door. "I'm sorry," she paused. "I don't even know your name."

"Ellen Boniface. You may call me Ellen."

Tania arrived back at Downsview in a mild state of shock. It had all happened so fast. In another week's time she was expected to move into Ellen Boniface's home and look after her, full time? They hadn't discussed hours, she hadn't seen her room, yet she had agreed on the spot. What had made her so reckless?

She had little time to consider her plight. Gloria was ready to serve dinner and the writer was already seated at one of the two small tables in the dining room.

Tania popped upstairs for a quick wash – there was no time to change – and then settled herself at the second table.

She glanced over at her fellow diner. He was tall and thin – a little younger than her, she guessed – with dark curly hair resting on his collar, and blue eyes in a pale face.

He was dressed completely in black.

He smiled at her. What would Tania Baker do in this situation? she thought.

"Good evening," she said, returning the smile.

"Did you have a good day?"

(Had Gloria told him about her?) "Interesting," she replied.

"That's good." He turned his attention to his meal.

He looks a bit like Dirk Bogarde,she thought but she

didn't speak again until Gloria brought their coffee.

"I'd better introduce myself properly. I'm John – and you are Tania? That's a pretty name."

And that's a bit feeble for a chat up line, she thought, but replied, "What do you write, John?"

"Oh, local history, mostly. Hey, would you be interested in a concert on Saturday night? It's on the organ – a Wurlitzer. If you haven't heard it it's worth going."

"I don't know. What kind of music?"

"All sorts – what do you like?"

What sort of music would Tania like? she thought. Barbara liked folk but they wouldn't play that on an organ.

"Music from the shows – anything with a strong melody," she said.

"That's perfect. Do say you'll come. It starts at 7.30. If we ask Gloria for an early tea we can leave here soon after seven. It isn't far."

"We can walk?"

"Yes. I do my exploring on foot or on a bike."

"That's what I'm going to do – explore. I've not seen much yet."

"I'll give you one of my books. That will tell you what to look for. That is – if you like history." He looked sheepish.

"I do – but I'll have to pay you for the book."

"Not at all. You might not like it and then you can give it back."

Tania giggled. He seemed so easy to talk to, and she was curious about his writing.

"I'll get it now," he said eagerly. "Just wait there."

Tania had no intention of moving and wasn't surprised when he sat down next to her and showed her his book.

It was beautifully produced, with lots of colourful illustrations.

"See, then and now," He bent forward. "But I must leave you to look at it without being a pest. I'll go and warn Gloria – and see you tomorrow. Goodnight."

Tania looked up as he turned away and felt sorry he hadn't stayed longer. Still, she had a date – something that gave her a warm excited feeling inside. Now she would have to decide what to wear. Goodness! It was almost like being a teenager again.

Next day Tania was out early searching for appropriate attire for an evening concert. She didn't want anything long. She didn't want to be overdressed – so she ignored the black velvet skirts and opted for an emerald green dress with an embroidered jacket. She also treated herself to a warm apricot winter coat – so different from the lilac fleece she had worn as Barbara. A new patent leather handbag and shoes completed the outfit.

She didn't have time for lunch at the hospital. She bought a local newspaper and a street map, a rather expensive shampoo and conditioner, and made her way home to prepare for her date.

While she was shopping all thoughts of her new job had been pushed to the back of her mind, but once she was home she began to regret her promise. She had accepted a position without knowing all the facts. She didn't know if she would like the house, her tasks or her employer. How could she have been so stupid?

Relax, she told herself – it was only a month's trial. If she wasn't happy she could leave, couldn't she? Meanwhile everything was turning out better than she had expected.

At least, it was – until she she saw John had dressed in a purple shirt with a bow tie! She had never dated a man who wore bow ties. What had she let herself in for?

As it turned out it was a very pleasant evening. John was charming and amusing – not too inquisitive but obviously interested in her. The music was enjoyable and her companion easy to talk to. She was beginning to think herself into her new persona, and feeling her horizons expanding.

He'd make a nice friend, she thought as she got ready for bed that night. I must keep in touch once I move.

She lingered over breakfast the next day but John did not appear. It was a cold, wet, miserable day and she forced herself to go out and buy an umbrella. She had a mediocre meal in one of department stores and came back to a dark and empty room.

It was the first time she had really felt lonely. She tried reading but regretted not buying a Sunday paper. Tony had always said they were a waste of money but one of the serious weekend offerings would have helped pass the time. Eventually she lay on the bed and fell asleep.

That evening she was assailed by doubts. She had given up so much. How could she tell whether it was worth it? She missed having someone else around – even if he had been most uncommunicative, and she missed fixing meals and watching television. Would Gloria mind if she bought a radio – or should she wait until she was in the new house?

After she'd been to have her ears pierced she would walk over to the street of tall houses and see if she could get round the back and find out more about the area.

She was surprised to find the houses in Cavendish Road had long gardens that backed onto the railway line. From the front they looked grand but she had to venture along a little row of tiny terraces to see into the gardens of the larger houses – and then there were so many trees she really couldn't tell what they were like. I need to get across the railway line and look from there, she thought and wandered towards the large car park bordering the line.

She was delighted to find there was a tunnel under the line and she walked through and followed the street back towards the railway. It was an industrial estate and the factories and offices blocked her view but eventually she found a stretch where she could see through the tall wire fence to the houses on the other side.

As befitted expensive properties they had extremely long gardens but she tried to count along to see which one was the back of Ellen's house. She wasn't sure. There were so many large trees bordering the line on the other side. She just hoped she wasn't expected to do any gardening as well as everything else.

Disappointed, she walked back into the park towards the hospital. Maybe she would feel happier if her new friend was there.

"Hallo, Tania," came a cheery greeting as they stood in line together.

"Hi, Fiona – am I glad to see you!"

"Why? What's happened?"

"I just had a miserable day yesterday – but I've got some news, too."

"Do tell."

"I'm moving into your road."

"You are? How?"

"Do you know Ellen Boniface?"

Fiona looked concerned. "You mean the old actress, two doors down from us?"

"Yes. What do you think of her?"

"She's a bit of a recluse. No-one really knows her. You aren't going to live there, are you?"

"Well, I have a month's trial – as a companion. She says she gets bored."

"I'm not surprised. From what I heard she doesn't have a TV or any electrical appliances in the house. I wish you luck."

"I had to get some kind of job – and you said yourself shop work was scarce."

"At least you'll be nice and near. Perhaps we could go out sometime, together?"

"You don't mind being seen with an old bird like me?"

"You aren't old."

They carried their trays to a table. As she sat down Fiona asked, "Have you just had your ears pierced?"

"Yes." Tania blushed.

"Wow. Just think what fun we could have choosing earrings together."

Tania felt herself laughing at the girl's enthusiasm. No matter how strange Ellen Boniface's home would be, she was beginning to feel comfortable about the changes she was making.

Four

Tony had to wait until Tuesday for the police to get back to him about the CCTV footage – but, when they did, it was worth it. They had found a sighting that matched Barbara's description and also another of her at Victoria. He went to the station and confirmed that it was his wife, although her hair seemed redder.

"She's wearing a wig!" he exclaimed.

"Yes, that's significant," said the officer with him. "It looks like she doesn't want to be recognised. I'm afraid if that is the case, there's nothing more we can do."

Tony fell silent. He didn't know what to say. He knew what they were thinking and he didn't want to react. Instead, he looked suitably crestfallen and made to leave.

"Let's hope she comes back of her own accord," said a policewoman, sympathetically. Tony couldn't wait to get out. He knew what he was going to do. He was going to London to find her himself.

He bought a cheap day return and sat planning his next move. He would cover all the hotels and B and B's near the station, showing them Barbara's picture and pretending to be her brother. His cover story would be that their mother was very ill and needed her. That should make them take notice.

At the third place he got lucky. They remembered a red headed lady who only stayed one night. She had bought some new luggage and left next morning, without a forwarding address. She had signed in as Barbara Hastings.

"What did she do with her old luggage?"

"She left us the case and took the bag with her. Sorry we can't be more help."

The case was the one his wife had taken. He thanked them and left.

Tony walked slowly back towards the station. The trail had gone cold. How did private detectives do this? He stopped by a parade of shops and glanced at the items for sale.

There was a rail of clothing just inside the door of a charity shop and one of the items of clothing looked familiar. It was a cream belted trench coat with brown buttons. His wife had been wearing that, but she must have discarded it. He sidled up to the display and felt in the pockets. They were empty.

"Excuse me," he said to the portly assistant behind the counter. "The lady who left the coat? Could you tell me if she left anything else?"

"Funny you should say that. She did leave a large

holdall but I'm afraid we sold it. It was empty. We always check."

"I don't suppose she said where she was going?"

"No – but she was heading towards the station, if that's any help."

It wasn't much help. He'd assumed Barbara would stay in London if she wanted to be lost in a crowd – but perhaps she had other ideas. He was no longer looking for a redhead in a mackintosh. He would have to go home and rethink his strategy. Where would she go that she would think he wouldn't follow?

As soon as he got home he rang Carole. He could hardly believe she knew nothing.

"Your mother was seen in London," he said. "I'm doing my best to find her. Have you any idea where she might have gone?"

"No – Dad."

"If she gets in touch you will tell me, won't you?"

"If she says it's OK."

"Please – can you think of any friends she might have gone to?"

"Not really. There was one, in Wales, but I don't know her name or where she lives."

"I don't think she's gone there. I think she went from Victoria. She wouldn't have stayed in Kent."

"Dad – trains from there cover an enormous area."

"I know – but I've nothing else to do. I'm going to find her."

"I'll let you know if I think of anything. Bye, Dad."

"Ta-ra."

*   *   *

He felt much better having spoken to his daughter. She even sounded as if she wanted to help. It was selfish of Barbara to take off and not let anyone know where she was going. What had got into the woman – letting her daughter worry about her like that? He would knock some sense into her when he found her. He'd been much too trusting. She could have gone off with anybody.

He had to consider the possiblity that she was unfaithful. Where would she go ,then? Brighton? It was as good a place as any to start. He'd wanted to see the new football stadium for some time. He'd go down for a week. It wouldn't be too expensive. He'd check when the Seagulls were playing at home. Even if he didn't find her he'd make sure he had a good time.

On Thursday Tania rang the bell at 24 Cavendish Road and waited for Ellen to answer. She looked flustered to see Tania on the doorstep. She was dressed in a long black gown and seemed to have lots of dark make-up on her eyes and her face was strangely white.

"I thought I'd better check to see if it was still all right to come tomorrow?" said Tania.

"Of course. Would you like to see your room?"

"Thank you."

Ellen led her up two flights of stairs and into a large room with a sloping ceiling.

"I'm afraid there isn't much furniture," she said, "but if you stay you can bring more. There's a bathroom and toilet on this floor and another room along the corridor for your use. I have made the bed. All the sheets are laundered every week, but you can bring your own if you would prefer."

"You send them away?"

"Yes. That's what I've always done."

"It looks perfect. What time do you expect me?"

"I'll be up by ten. I won't expect you to do much until the weekend. You'll need to get familiar with everything. I suppose you'll want one day a week free. How about Mondays?

"That would suit me."

"Thank you." Tania didn't really know how to respond. Should she act like an employee or a friend? This 'companion' business was very difficult. One thing she would need to do was to get some flat shoes. If she was going to be running up and down stairs her smart heels would not do.

Leaving the house, she hurried back to Downsview for her last proper meal. She and John had begun to share a table and she had enjoyed his company although he hadn't asked her out again.

"Give me your phone number," he'd said, but she hadn't bought a mobile phone yet.

"I'll ring when I get connected," she replied. She had the feeling it was going to be more important to have an address.

She bumped her cases up the steps to the front door of number 24 and rang the bell. Ellen looked smart in a mauve woollen suit and greeted her warmly.

"Come into the kitchen and I'll give you the keys," she said, with almost childlike enthusiasm.

Leaving her bags in the hall, Tania followed her down the long corridor to a door that stood ajar, revealing a room that didn't look as if had been changed since the 1950's.

There was a gas stove on one wall and a welsh dresser on the other. The open shelves were full of pots and pans and crockery. In the centre of the room was an enormous wooden table and, beside it, two stools. The windows beyond looked out over a stretch of lawn ending in what could be a vegetable patch.

Ellen pulled open a drawer in the table. "This is where we keep all the cutlery and in those cupboards you will find all the cleaning materials you need. If you wish to use anything not supplied please ask me first. There are some recipes in a book in the larder. If you use those until you are familiar with my requirements that should be satisfactory. We will, of course, eat together – except for breakfast which I have in my room.

I have ordered fish with chips to be delivered tonight at 6.30pm. I thought that would be a treat for us both. The fish is, of course, locally caught."

Tania couldn't decide whether her superior manner was natural or if she was putting on an act. If she starts ordering me about I won't stay, she thought.

However, once they sat down to eat in the elegant dining room Ellen was the perfect hostess. She laid the table, offered Tania wine or tea, the latter of which she accepted – and told her to choose from the fresh fruit in the bowl on the table for dessert.

They washed up together, Tania watching as Ellen put the dishes back where they belonged. She had the feeling it would not be wise to leave everything draining as she had at home.

"Would you like some music?" Ellen asked when they had finished.

"Yes, please," Tania answered, surprised – but when she followed Ellen into the front room she realised that, rather than records or a radio, she was intending to play the piano.

It turned out to be a companionable evening and Tania went to bed satisfied that she had made the right decision.

Tony thoroughly enjoyed the football match at the new stadium. He supported the home team and rejoiced with the rest when they won, two nil.

He had found a hotel on the outskirts of the town with a large car park and an easy bus ride to the town centre. The bar was full of geniality that evening and he relaxed in the warmth of friendly company.

A heavily made up young woman approached him near eleven and asked where he was from.

"London," he said, gruffly – his mood spoilt. Did he look as if he was in the market for sex?

She shrugged and left him to nurse the remains of his beer. He was reluctant to go to his room - he knew his task for the next day would not prove so enjoyable. But as people drifted away he dragged himself up the stairs, threw his clothes over a chair and climbed into bed.

The sheets were cold. 'If she stays away much longer I may be forced to find it elsewhere' he thought – but it didn't seem urgent. He was soon asleep.

His plan was to take Barbara's photograph to all the hotels in the area, while keeping a lookout in case she was out and about. He would use the, 'I'm her brother and her mother is ill,' cover story again, calling himself Paul Hastings.

In most places this worked but occasionally a receptionist would refuse to answer his questions. Maybe there was something about him that aroused their suspicions.

By lunch time he was ready for a drink and a rest but the first pub he came to had a distinctive 'boys together,' vibe so he took shelter in a restaurant overlooking the pier and ordered pie and mash and a coffee. Catching sight of himself in a mirror he felt a sense of shock. No wonder the people in the posh hotels thought him suspicious. Did he really look so wild and shabby? He would get a haircut, make sure he shaved for the evening and maybe look for a smarter jacket. After all, there were plenty of shops in Brighton and he could choose what he wanted without having to ask anyone else what they thought.

He found a navy jacket in a sale and spotted a blue roll-neck top that he fancied. That was enough for one day. He couldn't remember the last time he'd shopped for clothes. There didn't seem any point buying something new when he had perfectly good clothes in his wardrobe. However, he was beginning to realise that it was getting colder and the few items he had brought with him might not be suitable for a week by the coast.

The conversation in the bar that evening was of fishing and when Tony expressed an interest he was invited out in the boat the next day. It proved to be as productive as he had hoped and, though chilled, he was energised by the activity and the company.

Their catch was later taken home and he was urged to join them for supper. Arrangements were in hand for a bonfire evening the next night and Tony returned to the hotel with the warm glow of friendship that the skipper, Glen Rogers, and his wife had given him. He'd been invited to a family party and it had awakened memories of happier times. He would have to take a bottle or a six pack. For a fleeting second he wished Barbara was with him. Then he remembered why he was there. She probably wouldn't like his new friends anyway. He'd do his best to be sociable and start his search again in the morning.

Tired of tramping round Brighton he decided to drive to the next town. What did it matter whether he went west or east? He tossed a coin and it came up heads. He'd head west. He didn't hold out much hope. It was supposed to be a town of old folk but, then, Barbara was no spring chicken. He'd ask in the hotels and check out any fishing shops. He'd like to be more skilled with a rod, and to have his own equipment. He could practice by himself on the pier. Then he would feel like a real fisherman.

With no luck in the town's hotels he thought he'd try a few hair salons. She might be looking for work. No-one he asked had shown any interest in the photo but on the way back to the car park he noticed something familiar about a woman standing at a bus stop. She was about Barbara's height and build but he didn't recognise the clothes, or the short, blonde haircut. He started to cross the road but at that moment the bus drew up, obscuring his view, and by the time he had walked round behind it the doors had closed and it had started down the road.

"Where does that bus go?" he asked someone still waiting at the stop.

"That goes all along the coast, from East Sussex to Hampshire. Did you want to catch it?"

"No – it's not important." He felt a wave of disappointment. His expectations dashed- he wondered if he'd made a mistake. He hadn't had time – but his body was tingling with anticipation. It could have been Barbara – and if so – she was much nearer than he'd hoped.

He took his new rod and line back to the car. It seems his week was going to be nearer a fortnight.

Tania soon discovered why Ellen had offered her Monday off. It was her habit to go and get her hair set every Monday morning and she followed that with lunch at the pier. The evening meal would then be a salad.

The recipe book that Ellen had given her seemed to be basic British fare and most of the ingredients were in the larder or the big gas fridge that stood in the laundry room beside the kitchen. This also contained an old mangle and an ironing board.

'At least that's electric' thought Tania as, until that moment, the only electricity she had noticed was the lighting. There was no electric kettle, no microwave and very few sockets.

When she asked Ellen about this,as tactfully as she could, her companion just said, "I don't like rays in my house," and changed the subject.

She was always ready to talk about the past – especially her time in the theatre. "Not the West End – you understand, darling, but many provincial theatres."

She had a large scrap book of programmes and photographs, many of herself as the leading lady.

"Musical theatre was my forte," she claimed, "Especially, Hello Dolly."

"And pantomime?" encouraged Tania.

"There, look – I was a wonderful Wicked Witch of the West," she crowed as she turned the page.

'I'm not surprised,' thought Tania, wondering if she could broach the subject of exercise classes. Ellen seemed not to leave the house except for Mondays and Tania had discovered a pilates class at the local leisure centre. However, it was Wednesday afternoons and she wasn't sure that she would be allowed to go.

"Of course you can go, my dear," exclaimed Ellen when she asked her. "I don't intend to keep you locked up in this house. Some of my other companions even went out every night but that was most unsatisfactory. If you have an appointment or wish to go to the theatre or the cinema, just let me know in advance. I'll find something to do."

That weekend Tania discovered what Ellen really wanted her to do was play old fashioned games. She had a cupboard full of Snakes and Ladders, Ludo, Monopoly, Scrabble, cards, Draughts, Chess and even Trivial Pursuit.

While in the daytime she would do crossword puzzles or work on a large jigsaw she had laid out in the conservatory – in the evening she wanted Tania to get out one of the board games and play until one of them had won. She would not go to bed until the game ended, no matter what the time.

Tania soon found she couldn't beat Ellen at chess or scrabble, but when the results were mainly down to chance they were more evenly matched. Her main problem was sleeping after her brain had been stimulated. Even when they had cocoa together at eight thirty she still found it difficult to wind down before midnight.

Maybe it's being in a bed on my own, she thought, or not being physically tired?

Making breakfast was easy. Ellen came down and made flakes and a boiled egg most mornings and porridge on Sundays. She wore a long velvet housecoat and preferred it if Tania made herself scarce while she prepared her meal. Then she would take it upstairs and not come down again until much later. Tania bought some extra cereal, marmalade and juice and resigned herself to restricting herself to wholemeal bread or toast.

Lunch was usually soup, with a choice of cake or cheese and biscuits and dinner was often a casserole. Tania enjoyed preparing the meals and found it satisfying when Ellen complimented on her cooking. Sunday lunch was eaten late, after two o'clock, and Ellen liked her to read to her in the afternoon. "Something uplifting and classical," she would demand and Tania would try to find something she would enjoy, Jane Austen or Dickens.

Ellen did not allow her to do housework on the first floor. It was as if that level was to be kept private and that made Tania all the more curious. She was aware that Ellen's beauty regime included heavy layers of make-up that did not disguise the shrivelled state of her skin.

Her eyebrows were pencilled in and her lips a rich red – which she replenished after every meal.

Tania began to realise why the other workers had left. It wasn't so much that the duties were hard – they weren't much more than she had done in her own home – it was that Ellen was so demanding of attention. Crossword clues were read out loud and even jigsaw pieces discussed and discarded.

When Ellen wasn't being reminded of times past she was asking Tania questions about herself – questions that Barbara was reluctant to answer. She hadn't invented a past life for Tania but found herself having to do so, now.

Tania became the person she had always wanted to be – a woman with a loving husband who had died in a road accident. "He was a travelling salesman," she invented, "always bringing me back presents from the places he had visited."

"Didn't you ever go with him?"

"Oh, yes," and she would launch into memories from years ago.

Eventually the question that she had been dreading came, "Did you have any children, my dear?"

"No," Tania said, but she felt herself flush at the lie. "I lost a baby," she added – trying to cover up her embarrassment. It worked. Ellen asked no more, but it left Tania remembering the one person who she had not meant to hurt and wondering how she could ever justify her actions.

On Wednesday afternoon Tania set off for the Leisure Centre. It was too far to walk so she took the bus from the town centre. The class provided mats – but she wished she'd brought her own and vowed to purchase a thicker one.

At the end of the session some of the women congregated in the coffee bar to chat and Tania joined them. It was a relief to be out of the house, with people her own age. As long as she returned home by 5.30pm she would be in time to serve dinner.

Ellen was particularly inquisitive that evening – asking about the class and probing to see if Tania intended to continue with it.

In an effort to take the spotlight off herself Tania asked Ellen about her time on the stage. At once, games were forgotten and Ellen began reminiscing. She moved to the piano and began to sing.

"You have a lovely voice, Ellen," said Tania, "Were your parents musical?"

"Father was. He was a violinist with an orchestra. He went all over the country with them. Mother was different. She was frail. She kept falling asleep or complaining of aches and pains. I think he was glad to get away from her. He called it 'Ma's rheumatics,' and I think he believed she was putting it on."

"What did you think?"

"I don't know. They had very little to do with doctors – but I found that if I massaged her legs and sang to her it seemed to make her feel better. She didn't have anything much to stay alive for in the end. Father was either away or being very unsympathetic. I wasn't home all the time and she just faded away."

"Oh, Ellen, that's so sad."

"Then father got arthritis and couldn't play. He got very bad tempered and violent. It was not a good time. He was going to go into a home but he didn't want to go. I think he made himself ill. I found him on the bathroom floor." She shuddered. "But that wasn't what I was going to tell you about -wait here," and she left the room.

When she returned she had a large photo album with her. "I've not shown this to anyone for years," she whispered as she slowly turned the pages. When she paused over one photo of herself as a young woman Tania dared to ask, "Have you any other family, Ellen?"

"No, darling," Ellen looked wistful. "I have loved – but not wisely, I'm afraid. He belonged to someone else."

Now there were pictures of Ellen in costume, Ellen in a vintage car, "The London to Brighton Run," she laughed. "That was a wonderful day." Then Ellen in a publicity shot that showed an elegant, attractive woman, glowing with vitality and glamour.

"Wow!" exclaimed Tania, "You were a stunner."

"It's a long time ago." Ellen looked tired. "I think that's enough for now. Tomorrow I suppose we'll have to start planning for Christmas."

Tania shuddered. She hadn't realised this time of family unity was drawing close. A wave of guilt washed over her. She had to leave the room before Ellen saw how upset she was.

She hadn't cried since she left home but suddenly the enormity of what she had done swept over her. Nearly thirty years of her life had been dismissed, abandoned. It had seemed like an adventure but now it felt like a betrayal. She fell onto her bed and wept.

Five

Tania woke next morning with a new resolve. She had not given herself time to adjust to her new life. She would see the year out and then reassess the situation. She tried to imagine herself going back and couldn't. If everything she tried to do was made miserable by someone who would not, or could not, share her enthusiasm it was impossible to imagine herself living like that for ever.

When the song of a bird or the sight of a tree in blossom didn't stir him – when he wouldn't take her out for a meal because it was cheaper to eat at home -when she couldn't invite people round because he would either ignore them or be deliberately rude – when she tried to pacify him he just told her to shut up – there was no way she could return.

It was a relief to reach the following Monday, the day she was happy to think of as her day of freedom. She visited the library and joined, citing number 24 as her address. She changed one of her precious sovereigns in the jewellers, happy that she could afford presents for her friends. She rejected the idea of buying Christmas cards but she did look at the handbags in the department store before settling on a scarf for herself and another for Carole. She liked the idea that they might be wearing similar things this winter. Maybe by her actions she could show she still cared, even if she couldn't find the words. She would have to post it from some way away. That would be a trip for another Monday.

This week she was determined to go back to the hospital for lunch and, hopefully, meet Fiona.

She arrived early and there was no sign of her friend but she sat near the entrance and was rewarded by a wave and a breathless, "I'm so glad you're here. Father is coming out today. I can't stay for lunch."

"I'm glad about that," said Tania, and then laughed, "at your father's recovery, not that you'll miss lunch."

"Look, you must come round for tea one day. We are only at number 20. Can I call you?"

"I haven't got a mobile phone yet – but any Monday would be fine."

"Next week -say five o'clock? I must dash."

"Lovely, I'll see you then."

Fiona had made her think. Was it safe for her to get a pay-as-you-go phone with her new name and address? She didn't see why not. If no-one could connect her with Barbara Sharp what danger was there? She would do that this afternoon. Ellen need not know. She wouldn't like the idea of' 'rays' in her house but she also expected calls on the house phone to be for her, not Tania. Then, when had Tania ever heard the phone being used? Once

— the gardener had called to say it was too wet to mow the lawn.

She tried several shops before she found a phone she could understand. They had got far more complicated since she'd bought the one she'd left behind.

Then she wandered along the pier and tried some of the machines. 'I need somewhere to go this evening,' she thought, determined not to go back home. The obvious place was the pier pavilion. The entertainment that evening was a jazz band, with dinner,and she booked the last table available.

She didn't expect to enjoy it but it was surprisingly entertaining, if a little lonely. If she had been with someone else it would have made all the difference. Even Ellen would have been welcome, but she no longer liked loud music. There's a lot she doesn't like, thought Tania,but it was a job — and she was beginning to feel as though she belonged.

When she got back to the house that night Ellen was waiting up for her. "I'll make the cocoa," she said, "and you can tell me all about your day."

"I didn't do much," replied Tania. "I looked at the shops, went on the pier and stayed for an evening of jazz."

"Ah — the pier pavilion. I have sung and danced there plenty of times. I was the wicked queen in the pantomime Sleeping Beauty one year."

"Tell me about it," said Tania,craftily. She wasn't going to let Ellen know she had an invitation to the neighbours'.

Tony went home. He'd waited by the bus stop for two more days but the mysterious woman had not returned.

He tried to settle into his old routine – but the following Wednesday he drove down to the coast and waited by the bus stop again. The bus was another double decker but when it reached the stop there was no-one there who looked like Barbara.

He had brought a camera with him and glanced up at the windows as it pulled away. She was there! She was sitting in the back seat, talking to someone. She was different – but it could be Barbara. She must have got on at another stop. He couldn't get a photo this time but he'd come back next week. If it was her, she looked slimmer, happier. It hadn't occurred to him before that he hadn't heard her laugh for a long while. What was it that could be making her look so cheerful? Jealousy made him bitter. She'd thought she could get away but he'd found her now. It wouldn't be long before he'd have her back home.

Yet the idea didn't have the appeal it once had. What was there at home for them? He shook off the question and drove over to Brighton to see his new friends.

A convivial evening in the pub relaxed him and when they invited him to stay the night he accepted. If he lived down here, he thought, he'd be a lot happier – but property prices made it impossible – especially when he had no job and no prospect of getting one.

Back in Kent he felt he had to tell someone what he had discovered. He rang his daughter. "Carole," he said, "I think I know where your mother is."

"That's great, Dad. Where?"

"Down on the South coast. I've seen someone who looks like her."

"Did you talk to her?"

"No. She was on a bus. I'm going back there next week."

"Take it slowly, Dad. Let her explain. You want her to come back, don't you?"

"Of course, if it really is her. I can't believe she did this."

"I wish I could be there to help. Good luck, Dad."

"OK. I'll talk again soon, when I've got more news." He rang off.

The next Wednesday he was again on the road south. This time he would park up early and get on the blessed bus himself. That should solve the problem for once and for all.

But it didn't. Barbara was not on the bus. He went a few stops, checking upstairs and down, and then got off. He didn't think it was too far to walk back. He'd get a drink on the way and then go home. He wasn't in the mood to meet his friends.

He drove out of the car park and into traffic, over a roundabout and onto the dual carriageway. He could go faster now and began to get irritated as other drivers seemed to block his way.

"Move over, you stupid bugger," he shouted at a white van.

Coming to another roundabout he sped into it, went to turn off – and slammed into a car which had braked suddenly in front of him. It wasn't a bad crunch, but it was followed by a hefty thump from behind. With no time to congratulate himself on his quick reactions, and with a startled "What the.." Tony was flung forward – his air bag inflated and he passed out.

* * *

The tea that Tania had with Fiona and her father was a delight. The hall had regency striped wallpaper and coved ceilings. All the woodwork was white – as were the walls of the kitchen, with pine cupboards and blue and white checked curtains.

"I hope you don't mind," said Fiona, "We eat in the kitchen."

"It's lovely," said Tania, "and what a spread!"

"Here's father. Dad, this is Tania."

Tania held out her hand. "Pleased to meet you, Mr?"

"Davies – but you can call me Ted."

He was about her height, she thought, but broader – with a slight stoop, silver white hair and blue twinkly eyes.

"Sit down, please – and help yourself," he said, pulling up a chair next to hers.

Sandwiches, salad, pate, toast, scones and cake, yoghurt and fruit – Tania relaxed in the warmth of their welcome.

They were curious about her work with Ellen Boniface and she responded by grilling them about the old lady's past and the changes they had seen over the years.

The house was her parental home, although she was often absent, as was her father while he was playing in the orchestras, she learnt. Unfortunately when he became arthritic and returned home permanently his wife became ill and the house became neglected.

"Did they have anything modern in the house?"

"I'm sure they did. Certainly they had radio and TV when her mother was alive but her father became paranoid about the outside world. He would never go to see her perform, even when she was in town."

"Did she talk to you?"

"Not me," said Fiona, "but she did speak to Mum sometimes."

"Gladys was very sorry for her," said Ted. "She felt she wanted to be anyone but herself. She's not got much of a life, has she?"

"Once her mother died she had to look after her father by herself and give up her career. I think the two of them drove each other a little mad. We saw less and less of her and when my wife passed on, all contact ceased. Maybe we were wrong."

"It does explain why Ellen seemed so lonely. I suppose I'd better go back. That was a lovely meal, thank you."

"Don't go yet. Stay and watch a video with us. I can't imagine life without a TV now."

"Well, I don't have to be there for dinner." Tania wavered.

"Nature, comedy or a musical?"

"Comedy, please."

"Right, Morecambe and Wise."

So they spent the evening laughing together and it was the best few hours Tania had had for many years.

Tony woke up with blurred vision and a headache. He was in a bed. The place had the odour of disinfectant. His leg felt strange and his neck was in a brace. He blinked, trying to remember what had happened.

There was someone standing by his bed. A red faced, bearded man.

"Father Christmas?" Tony exclaimed.

"Oh, hang out the flags. Tony's made a joke!" his friend replied.

"I'm in a hospital?"

"Yep."

"The car?"

"A write off."

"Damn. What happened?"

"A shunt. You came off worst."

"Nobody died?"

"No."

"Thank God."

"Yep."

"What are you doing here?"

"They found the address of the hotel in your wallet. They rang to see if you were staying there and Richard told me where you were. The boys wish you well. They delegated me to be the first visitor."

"I'd rather see Marge."

"I bet you would."

"How long have I been here, Glen?"

"Only two days. Why? You need to be somewhere?"

"Not really." He shifted his head on the pillow. "I guess I had whiplash."

"Yep. - and broken a bone in one leg, but you seem as bright as usual."

Tony winced. That was the first time anyone had called him bright – and he didn't feel it, but he was grateful that Glen was trying to cheer him up.

"Well, I'd better be off. I'll tell Marge to bring you in some grapes, shall I?"

"And a bottle."

"Some hopes!"

Tony tried to turn his head but couldn't. He shifted his

buttocks and felt a sharp pain in his leg. Now his friend had gone he felt the light hurting his eyes and his brain felt like lead. Where were the nurses? Surely they could give him a painkiller, and a drink? He was very thirsty.

"Nurse!" he croaked and saw a curtain move at the corner of his vision.

"Ah, Mr Sharp. Your visitor said you were awake. If I sit you up can you take a drink?"

"Yes, please. My head feels odd."

"You had concussion."

"That's why I saw stars. I had a very strange dream. I was in Germany, at a Christmas market and there was a cow bell ringing and ringing and it wouldn't stop. In the end I tripped over the stalls and the stall holders were chasing me and I woke up."

"Well, you're here now and we're going to get you better. Here's some water and if you keep that down you can have a cup of tea later."

She bent over him and he caught a faint scent of honeysuckle. She was very pretty and he felt a sudden urge to kiss her but he could hardly move his head as she tipped the end of the bed and lifted him under the arms so he could sit up to drink.

Six

Carole Sharp put the phone down and stood irresolute. She might have expected something like this but she'd been so involved with her own problems she hadn't considered what was happening with her parents.

For years she'd lived happily with her mother – seeing her father only as an intermittent interruption to their lives. He was someone who came home bringing gifts and making their small home seem smaller and noisier than when he was away. She found his presence loving but intimidating – as if he was unsure how to deal with a daughter in the family, and Mother hadn't helped. It was as if she'd wanted to keep Carole to herself and not let anyone intrude on their organised lives.

It was when she got a place at University that she'd begun to feel a stranger in her own home. They'd said they were proud of her but couldn't understand her choice of Durham.

"You could study Geography anywhere," her father

had grumbled, but her mother just went quiet.

She didn't dare tell them the atmosphere was so cool at home she longed to get as far away from them as possible.

She had succeeded – both academically and socially and felt so at home in the North that she'd found work as an estate agent and stayed in the area. Visits home were infrequent, Christmas and once in the summer, and when her father was made redundant even those stopped.

There was another reason. She had fallen in love with her boss. Working together they had found they had the same sense of humour and similar tastes in properties. Carole knew when he sent her to see a tiny flat, a few miles north of the town, he had chosen it because he felt she would like it.

"You can't stay in lodgings for ever," he'd said. "Let's furnish it together."

But there was a problem. He hadn't kept it a secret. She knew he was married.

"As soon as the boys are old enough I'll tell them about us," he'd said. "She doesn't love me any more. We even have single beds."

Carole wasn't surprised. She'd seen photographs of his wife at a Christmas party and was amazed that such an elegant man was married to a woman who could only be described as an apple on legs.

"She's never been happy," he'd explained, "but the more she eats, the more miserable she gets."

They were discreet, of course. They only met when he could plead work commitments. His sons were eight and ten. She didn't know when he'd think they were old enough to understand.

She just knew that she had never known anyone as kind, amusing and inventive as he was. He'd find a tiny pub out in the country for an evening meal. They went fishing together, and into North Yorkshire for walking and sightseeing. They had rides on railways that she hadn't known existed and traipsed over moors where the grouse ran out of the heather squeaking alarm.

They bought paintings of the area by a local artist and hung them in the flat. It became their haven and, although he rarely stayed the night, Carole was happier than she had ever been.

It was only when the inevitable happened that her dream turned sour.

She began to lose concentration at work and lost them a promising sale. Then she became ill and the sickness alerted her to the possibility. A test from the chemist confirmed that she was pregnant. She couldn't believe they had been so careless. Then she remembered the one time she had forgotten her pill. She had pushed it to the back of her mind, not telling Paul and trusting that nothing would happen.

At first she couldn't tell him. Each time she planned to break the news he seemed so happy and loving that she couldn't spoil the mood.

Then, one day, she slipped on the steps up to the flat.

"The rail's broken," he said. "We'll have to get it fixed. Are you OK?"

It was the opening she had been waiting for. "Not really."

"What's up? I thought you'd been looking a bit peaky."

"Come inside. I need to sit down."

Once they were seated together on the sofa she didn't know how to start. She looked at his face and saw a worried frown appear. Grabbing his hands before he had time to speak she said, "Paul. I'm going to have a baby."

She felt his fingers twitch as he took a deep breath. "Are you sure?"

"Yes, I did a test – but I'm going to see the doctor to make certain."

"Poor love."

He was staring at her as if she was a stranger. Then, with a loud sigh, he continued,

"Still, you're young. There'll be plenty of time for more babies."

"What do you mean? You don't...."

"Think about it, Carole. You can't bring up a baby on your own."

He reached out to her at last, gripping her arms to emphasise his argument.

She shook her head in disbelief. "I didn't think I'd have to."

"My darling. One family is enough for any man."

"Do you honestly believe I'd have an abortion?"

"After due deliberation. I recognise it isn't the easiest option."

"Isn't the easiest option! It's our baby, yours and mine – don't you feel that means anything?"

"Of course it does." He tried to put his arm round her shoulders. "I would love to have a baby with you – but not now – not yet. Be reasonable, Carole."

"Do you know something? For once I don't believe you. That charm you use on all our customers I thought was genuine. You made me so happy. Now I think you'd better go."

"You'll be at work tomorrow?"

"Oh yes, you bet. After all, I'll need the money, won't I – if I'm to be a single mum?"

He bent to kiss her but she turned her head away. There was a flash of unaccustomed anger in his eyes as he left the flat.

She sat, drained – too exhausted to cry. She wanted her mother, but her mother had run away. She curled up in a ball, waiting for the ache in her chest to fade. So this is was what it felt like to be broken hearted. She wanted to get up and smash everything they had bought together, but she didn't. She rose unsteadily, went into the kitchen and made a large mug of old fashioned cocoa.

Tomorrow she would go to see the doctor and find out when the baby was due. The flat was hers as long as she could afford it. Paul had only helped to buy the contents. Had he known, even then, that he was never going to leave his wife?

She couldn't believe that he'd felt nothing for her all the months they had been together. What a fool she'd been – and what would her father say? Now was not the time to tell him. They had to find her mother first. She would surely be happy to be a grandmother. Tears came at last and she went to bed hoping her misery was not detectable by the baby in her womb.

Tania was beginning to feel suffocated. One day and one afternoon a week away from the house was not enough. She had tried making friends with the other women at the pilates class but they either had families or they met for coffee and shopping trips on other days when she wasn't free.

Ellen, too, was behaving more and more strangely. She would break off in the middle of a conversation and seem to go into a trance. Sometimes she would call Tania 'mother' and at other times seem to be dreading the coming festivities.

Tania also began to dread the so-called season of goodwill. She had received a few cards, from people she had met since she'd come to the town, but what she really longed for was contact with her daughter. She'd thought she could disappear and become a different person but there was no way she could cut off all contact with her daughter. She wanted to explain why she had left and what a difference being apart from Tony had made. She wanted to reassure Carole that it had nothing to do with her and if she'd been sure she wouldn't tell her father where she was she would have confided in her.

Eventually she could bear it no longer. She took a bus inland and rang Carole from her new mobile phone. There was no reply.

Tania looked at the brightly decorated shops and felt crushed, diminished, by the bustling crowds of people. She had intended to look for a present for Ellen – and something for Fiona and her father, but how could she shop when she felt so miserable and alone?

There was a biting wind and she took shelter in a large department store. There she found a tartan scarf for Ted and a jewellery box for Fiona. For Ellen she bought an expensive canteen of cutlery. She didn't know why she felt drawn to it. She only knew the pieces she'd been using in the house were quite old and some had loose handles. She was afraid the old lady might be insulted as it was not a personal present, so she added a box of liqueur chocolates.

Finally she treated herself to a set of DVDs -a historical drama, hoping that the Davies family would let her play them sometime. Of course, the answer would be to get a laptop computer of her own, but she didn't know how she could use one without Ellen finding out.

At the end of her probationary month Ellen had told her how much difference she had made to her life and how grateful she was that Tania had come to live with her. She had even hinted that she was becoming fond of her companion and that Tania was 'more precious' than anyone else in her life.

Tania began to feel uncomfortable. She could easily get accused of influencing the old lady. She wanted nothing more than a job and the chance to carve out a new life for herself – but somehow she had been absorbed into Ellen's strange world and felt herself unable to grow into a new identity.

There was also the puzzle of the first floor. Why did Ellen not let anyone else go up there? What was so private, so secret, that only she was allowed to see it?

Tania was tormented with the possibilities. Was there a wardrobe full of old costumes? Was there a shrine to one or other of her parents? Was there a room she had kept just as she had used it as a child? Or maybe it was just another bathroom where she tried to recapture her youth.

It began to weigh on Tania's mind until she determined that at the next opportunity she would venture into the forbidden territory and see what it was that Ellen would not let anyone else see.

The Monday before Christmas she had her chance. Ellen had gone to the hairdressers as usual and Tania came back to the house, let herself in and climbed the stairs to the first floor. Her heart was thumping and she felt a strange tingling in her scalp. She rubbed the sweat off her palms and stood on the silent landing wondering which of the four doors to open first. The first door on the right was the nearest. She opened it and found herself in a rose pink bathroom. There was no shower but a large enamel bath with gleaming chrome taps. Ellen certainly looked after this room! Seeing nothing untoward she moved to the next door. It was at the back of the house and turned out to be Ellen's bedroom and the style was fascinating. It actually had tapestries on the walls! The bed was large, but reasonably modern and the dressing table was covered with pots, jars, dishes and ornaments. Beside the bed was a breakfast table and the wooden cupboards were light and edged with gold. The gold curtained windows looked over the garden to the trees that hid the railway. It was a strange room, but not unpleasant. It felt like a room that was trying to be both antique and modern, artistic and practical, rather like Ellen herself.

Tania examined the tapestries. They had an oriental feel – scenes of trees, rivers, animals and little houses, rather like the willow pattern design, but in muted browns, blues and reds.

The room smelled of perfume and spices. It was exotic but welcoming.

Shutting the door swiftly she left the bedroom and went to open the third door. The corridor was in darkness now, and she expected to see light inside but, instead, she felt a cold draught that made her shiver. To her surprise the darkness was even more intense and there was a strange smell that she could not identify. It seemed this was not the entrance to a room, but a cupboard. She took a tentative step forward and her face brushed against something soft. It felt like hair – and brought goosebumps to her skin. There was something about this place that made her skin crawl and her pulse race. Whatever it was, she didn't stay to discover. She turned back to the half open door and rushed through, pulling it firmly behind her. She stood in the corridor, shaking and trying not to cry. What kind of creature had she discovered?

She could hardly breathe with the choking sensation of fear. Nothing had prepared her for this. She leaned against the wall, her legs weak and her breathing rushed, until a slam of the front door indicated that Ellen had returned. Tania would be required to go down and converse with her and finalise the arrangements for Christmas day. She shuddered. How was she ever going to enjoy herself now?

Ellen had ordered a large real Christmas tree but, to Tania's surprise, did not decorate it in the usual manner. She had known Ellen would not want fairy lights but she hadn't expected the only coverings allowed would be cotton wool and silver tinsel. Tania had little time to rationalise what she had seen. Instead, she rang her daughter again on Christmas Eve. There was no answer from the flat and her mobile went to messages.

"Happy Christmas, darling," said Tania, "I haven't forgotten you and I love you very much. I'll talk to you in the New Year. I'm sorry I couldn't stay with your father. Please don't give him this number."

She rang off. There was nothing else to say.

Seven

Carole had sold the flat. It was easy to move the mortgage while she was still working full time. Paul had arranged for her transfer to Bishop Auckland as she had requested and no-one yet knew that she was pregnant.

The tiny terraced house with a patio garden had only cost half what a similar home would be in the south. She had chosen it for its proximity to the shops and the park. She was determined to bring up her child in the caring, simple style that the town seemed to embody. It wasn't full of students and tourists like Durham – but it wasn't derelict and abandoned like some other pit villages. She was sure she could be happy there.

The call from her mother was a surprise. She didn't say much and Carole was left wondering what she was doing with her life now she had left Carole's father. How much could she say to her mother without seeming disloyal to her father? After all it was her mother who had left. She'd been willing to cut out everyone in her old life. It would serve her right if she didn't hear from her daughter for a while.It was very confusing. While her feelings about men in general had hardened she was still concerned that Barbara was not aware that Tony was on her trail. She didn't know whether to tell her or not and decided to wait until after Christmas and see how her father fared. He seemed to be in the right place, with his friends, and he hadn't mentioned her mother in the last call she had had from him.

She didn't bother with a landline in her new home. She would rely on her mobile. The only decision she had to make now was whether to go south for the new year or stay where she was.

In the end the decision was made for her. She was so sick she had felt weak all day, too weak to travel south. She kept up appearances in the office, there really wasn't much work in the winter months, and then went home and nibbled dry toast and apricots at night. It was a strange craving but she supposed it was what her body needed.

The hospital wasn't far away and she booked her scan and waited. Paul had sent her a large bunch of flowers at Christmas, (temporary, like you, she thought bitterly) The message read "Welcome to Your New Home, Paul."

Tony spent Christmas in hospital. The Brighton football team came round the wards, really to see the children, but he was on crutches by then and managed to spot two of them. The Christmas dinner was surprisingly good and a number of the fishermen dropped in that evening to wish him well.

"I'll be out soon," he claimed, "Just staying put while the weather's bad."

The nurses had asked him if he had anyone at home to help him when he was discharged.

"No," he admitted reluctantly. "My family are all away." He'd put Carole as his next of kin and finally felt ready to tell her of his misfortune. Perhaps she would come down for a while and look after him? That evening he rang her mobile and she answered straight away.

"Hallo, Dad. Did you get your Christmas present?" she asked.

"No. I'm sorry darling. I'm not at home. I'm in hospital. Don't worry, I'm OK."

"What's wrong? What happened? Where are you?"

"I'm in Brighton. The car had a knock. I hurt my leg but it's getting better. They say I can come out if I have someone to look after me."

"Oh, Dad. I would if I could. Maybe I could get a few days. Would that be enough? How are you feeling?"

"I'm fine. Your old man's a tough old stick – but I've got no transport. All that needs sorting out."

"I've changed offices, Dad . I'm also changing my mobile. I'll text the new number. Ring the same time tomorrow and I'll see what I can arrange. Love you."

Tony blinked. When was the last time anyone told him they loved him? Years ago. It was almost worth getting smashed up to hear his daughter say that.

Ellen was insistent. There was to be no special Christmas dinner. Lunch would be soup, maybe with a mince pie to follow, and they could have roast chicken for dinner but the day would be spent as usual, with half an hour set aside for opening the few presents that were arranged under the tree.

The gift from Ellen was larger than she had expected. The big, soft parcel contained a floral duvet, something she had longed for since her bedroom was cold at night.

"Thank you, Ellen. That's very generous," she said.

"I'll open mine now, shall I?"

Tania watched with trepidation as Ellen tore off the paper. She tried to analyse the expression on her face and was relieved when Ellen smiled broadly.

"Wonderful. What a beautiful choice – so classical. It will be hard to give up the old knives and forks but perhaps we could keep these for dinner time. Thank you, Tania."

The other parcels were a box of fruit jellies for Ellen and a book for Tania from Fiona and Ted. The final parcel was a new jigsaw puzzle that Ellen must have chosen for herself and Tania was angry for not thinking of it. Ellen put it to one side. "Monopoly, today, I think," she said and they played board games until tea time.

Tania couldn't help thinking of the Christmasses she had spent with Tony and Carole when she was young. This was a strange way to spend a day that was meant for families. Yet Ellen deserved to have an enjoyable time and she was glad she could provide it.

Next day Tania went round to Fiona's to thank her for the present, but only stayed a short while. Ted seemed tired and preoccupied. Tania couldn't tell them about the horror behind the door upstairs. She had tried to reason herself out of her fears but the more she thought about it, the more certain she became that Ellen had hidden some kind of animal in the house. Yet the cupboard didn't smell of animal, and what animal was as tall as she was? There was also the chill that made her think there was something else going on. She didn't believe in ghosts but it reminded her of the stories of ethereal spirits that ghost hunters went to search for in haunted houses. She would have to find the courage to return. Meanwhile she would be more alert and try to see if food disappeared from the kitchen.

Carole came down as promised and picked her father up from the hospital, taking him home to Kent. Then, one evening, she told him about the baby.

"You're pregnant? I didn't even know you were seeing anyone. Are you getting married?"

"We can't, Dad. He's already got a wife."

"You stupid idiot! How will you cope with a baby?"

"I've bought a house. I'm still working. It is possible, Dad."

"When's it due?"

"April."

"Your mother would love to know she's going to be a granny."

"And you'll be a granddad. How'll that feel?"

Tony shrugged. "Haven't I got enough to worry about? There's a new car to get, don't forget."

"Well, don't worry about me. It's much cheaper living up there."

Tony went silent. He was staring at the room as if he was trying to make a decision. "This house is a bit big for me without your mother" he muttered. "It would serve the silly cow right if I sold it."

"Stop it, Dad. She may still come back." Carole didn't say any more and hoped her face didn't give her away. She really ought to ring her mother. The longer she left it the harder it would be to know what to say.

"I don't know. I really don't know." Tony was muttering.

It was a subdued Tony that let his daughter take care of things for a few days and once she had gone he made it his prime task to find a small car and set off once more for the south coast. Not only did he wish to find Barbara but he could see other possibilities that could transform his life.

Tania's plans for further investigation of the first floor had suffered a setback

Ellen was sick. She had retired to bed and finally allowed Tania to enter her bedroom to take care of her. She was not an easy patient and demanded frequent drinks of lemon and honey and a change of hot water bottle every two hours. After much discussion she had accepted that she needed to see a doctor and it was while she was thus occupied that Tania tried the door that she still considered should lead to another room. It was locked. Ellen must have begun locking it as soon as she allowed Tania upstairs.

"Rest, warmth and plenty to drink," was the prescription. "Let me know if she has difficulty breathing or shows signs of getting worse," said the doctor as he left. "She's lucky to have you to look after her."

"Thank you, doctor. I will," replied Tania. That was

something else she needed to do, register with a doctor. Could she do it without any previous medical records? What could she say if she was asked about her past? She hadn't dared find a dentist either. People were identified by their dental records after they had died – weren't they? Why was she thinking about death? Was there something living in the house that was dangerous? Should she confess to Ellen that she knew it was there?

No, first of all she would explore the final room. That might answer some of her questions. She hoped Ellen hadn't locked that door, too.

By the middle of January Ellen was back to her old self. Tania had waited until she could be sure she was out of the house before she ventured into the final room on the first floor.

Ellen had seemed relieved that all signs of Christmas had gone and had even expressed delight at a sudden snowfall that had left the garden looking pristine.

She ordered a taxi to take her into town and Tania could have sworn that she was holding herself more upright and wearing an even brighter red lipstick than usual. It was almost as if she was witnessing some kind of transformation. Perhaps the new year had given Ellen new life or, at least, a determination to make the best of the old one.

Tania took a torch and mounted the stairs, passing the mystery door and trying the handle of the last front room. It opened easily and the light from the window showed two walls of fitted cupboards. She tried the light switch and the extra light revealed a full length mirror on one door. This was more the kind of room Tania had expected and her impressions were confirmed when, opening the first cupboard, she found a row of full length costumes. There were velvet cloaks, some trimmed with fur; long, sequinned dresses; silver and white jackets and long white boots. In the next wardrobe she found scarlet and purple outfits, some with dragons and fanciful creatures embroidered on them and, hanging opposite, a range of black dresses and cloaks. The final cupboard had hats and gloves, tall pointed witches hats, gold and silver crowns and even an oriental hat, brightly coloured and seemingly out of place among the other headgear.

These must be costumes from her shows, thought Tania. She was amazed that Ellen had been allowed to keep them. However – there was no obvious clue as to what was happening in the mystery room.

She couldn't leave the floor without trying once more to see what was behind the door. All had been silent when she tried before. She would try the door, but this time she would stand back and shine the torch ahead of her.

To her surprise the handle turned and the door opened. Slowly she pushed it a little further, then waited to see if anything stirred. When nothing happened she switched on the torch and, with one hand still on the door handle, shone the light into the space.

At first she thought she had made a mistake and opened the wrong door. What was this smooth, silky hair she could feel? She gave a sigh of relief as she realised it was fur coats – thick fur coats, hanging from a pole above her head and so tightly packed that she couldn't see beyond them into the room.

She gave a nervous giggle. Fancy being afraid of a few fur coats! Then she pushed one aside, feeling it rock on the hanger as she did so and, leaving the door behind her, moved forward. Her face brushed up against a sleeve and, for a moment, she felt a shiver of alarm. Then, telling herself not to be so silly, she pushed on, through the coats and into the room.

The walls were painted white and the bare floorboards creaked as she stepped forwards. Before her were ranged four rows of assorted chairs, dining chairs, garden chairs and even one armchair. They looked like they had been collected from jumble sales. The rows of chairs faced a makeshift stage, wooden boards set on pallets, which had part of a medieval stage set arranged across the back – a grey stone castle with slit windows. On the centre of the stage was a long dark table laid with wooden platters.

At the head of the table stood an ornate throne, seemingly covered in precious stones, glowing red, green and gold in the dim light from the the front window, which was curtained by fold of pure white voile, fluttering slightly as if in a draught.

But the most unsettling thing about the scene was that the front row was occupied by three figures.

They appeared to be one man and two women. They were sitting absolutely still. As still, thought Tania, as corpses. Surely they could not be real?

She looked behind her at the dark fur coats, still swinging slightly as she let them go. Dare she examine the figures? What if they were really dead? Could she imagine Ellen placing them there so that she could have an audience for her performance? Unfortunately she could.

She took one step towards them – and then another. For some reason she felt it important to be as quiet as possible.

When she grew level with the front row she stopped and scrutinised the first figure.

It was a woman – a very smartly dressed woman with a green coat and a little hat with a feather – but the face was pale and smooth with bright red lipstick and blue expressionless eyes. It was a mannequin – a doll – not a person at all.

Tania felt her body relax and went to the front of the row. Sure enough, the other two figures were also mannequins – dressed as if they had just come from a shop window. She stifled a giggle. Ellen must really have missed being on the stage to make this imitation theatre and act out her fantasies.

She turned her attention to the makeshift stage. It had a real backcloth and scenery, painted to be a magical looking grey stone castle, like something from Sleeping Beauty.

Before it the heavy, antique table arranged as if for a banquet.

Tania shuddered. The whole scene felt like some Alice in Wonderland nightmare. Of course, if someone opened the door casually they would think it was a cupboard and not venture to go further. So this was what Ellen kept secret. Did she spend her time when she wasn't with Tania like a regal Miss Havisham, lording it over an imaginary feast?

Tania felt a tide of sadness wash over her. How terrible to have so little in this life that she had to invent another.

And yet – wasn't that what Tania was trying to do?

The wind made the curtains flap and she heard a soft growl. The sound seemed to come from behind the stage set. Could there really be something alive in that room – something that knew she should not be there? The growl came again and she flung herself at the door, rattling the hangers, pushed it open, turned and slammed it shut. All that time spent convincing herself that there was nothing to be afraid of – ruined by one little growl!

If, as she suspected, Ellen was acting as a wicked queen or even a witch, maybe she kept some kind of familiar in the room. Everything had seemed so normal in this house – old fashioned, yes, but not supernatural! And now events had her imagining fearsome creatures and frightening herself with suspicions about her housemate. Yet she couldn't think of Ellen as wicked. She might be bossy but she didn't seem spiteful. Still, there was certainly something different about her.

As Tania's heart slowed down she tried to focus on the sound she had heard. It had come, she believed, from low down. What kind of animal could be living in that room? She would never know. Could she ever dare to go back?

That evening Tania thought back to the life she had envisaged when she ran away. Nothing had turned out as she had expected. She had imagined herself as a free agent, able to choose where to live, what to do and how to spend her time. She had thought she would find new friends who shared her interests and, most of all, she would find respect for herself as an individual.

Instead she had bound herself to a stranger, one who needed her, to be sure, but one who restricted her, took up her time, dictated her interests and made her feel inferior. She felt obliged to stay, at least until the mystery of the strange room was solved, but she was beginning to regret her decision.

Eight

Tony was frustrated. Once again there had been no sign of the woman he thought was his wife on the Wednesday bus. He was ready to give up. He would turn his attention to researching jobs in the area and looking at the kind of home he could live in without Barbara. He had passed a mobile home site that looked promising, although he knew most of them only allowed usage for nine months of the year. Nevertheless he believed some were residential and began to make enquiries.

He joined his friends in the pub and told them his plans.

"You'll be right on the beach," said Glen, jealously. "Next thing you'll be wanting a boat."

"One day, perhaps," replied Tony. "At first I'll stick to beach casting. At least it will be handy for digging up bait.."

"Are there any places for sale?" was the next question.

"One, but I've not seen it. I haven't put my own house on the market yet. I don't know how long it will take to sell."

"Spring is the right time, mate. Good luck to you."

But Tony didn't feel lucky. Actually, he felt lonely – but he would never admit it.

Barbara would have been so much better at getting the house ready for viewers.

He hadn't realised how many memories they had stored in the attic – photograph albums full of pictures of their honeymoon, of baby Carole and all stages of her growing up.

Barbara had also kept postcards of places they had visited together and he had to smile at the reminders of strange hotels where they had made love in tiny single beds and walked the streets together looking for presents to take home for her mother. They were happy times and he wondered why things had gone so wrong. It was just, he thought, that his life had got so narrow. No-one needed him for anything. He couldn't understand people who said retirement was the best time of their lives. He'd been existing on auto pilot and now he was forced to accept the need for change he found it a bewildering sensation.

He still played darts regularly. He even began to get more adventurous about his breakfasts – trying new coffees and different cereals. It wasn't much – but it made him feel in control.

It was when it came to the home, and seeing it with the eyes of a prospective purchaser, that he felt daunted. Eventually he took the estate agent's advice. He painted all the walls with neutral colours – magnolia, pale green and peach. Then he went over the white woodwork, freshening it up where necessary, and had the carpets cleaned.

As the house was transformed he began to feel quite proud of it and,once he turned his attention to the garden,he began to relax. He'd always insisted on a neat lawn and as he pruned the bushes and checked the fences he rediscovered a feeling of peace that he had forgotten he'd ever experienced.

He began to treat himself to a rum and coke or a whisky on the nights he felt he'd achieved something. It didn't make up for the fact that Barbara was not with him but it gave him a quick flash of superiority. He was managing without her – at least until he reached his cold and empty bed.

The estate agent had booked two prospective buyers for viewings at the weekend. Tony was irritated. It would mean his whole morning would be taken up with visitors. He didn't trust the estate agent to take anyone round on his own. He wanted to be there to see how they viewed the property and whether they were genuine or time wasters.

The first couple were newly weds and he got the impression they had already seen the house they wanted but, later, as the second couple went round, and he heard the wife saying how beautiful everything was, and how the kitchen was just as she would have designed it, he began to realise that this could be a sale. Finally, when the agent took him to one side and explained that there would be no chain as they were at present renting, seemingly wanting him to agree then and there, he pushed past them, muttering "must go out," and sped down the path leaving the astonished trio behind him.

He walked fast, not thinking where he was going – just trying to clear the throbbing in his head until, hot and breathless, he found himself at the entrance to the cemetery.

He gave a bitter laugh and paused – then walked slowly through the entrance and along the path between the graves. The edge of the path was lined with crocus, purple, yellow and white, and the sense of order and peace slowly began to calm him.

He reached a wooden bench and sat in the sunshine, listening to the birds and trying to stop tears coming to his eyes.

He might as well be dead. Without Barbara, who was there to care whether he lived or died? Why had she stopped caring? Was there someone new in her life? Was he too old to find someone else and start all over again?

He tried to focus on his plans for the future but they seemed to slip away from him. He needed to discuss them with someone to be sure he was doing the right thing. He wanted the reassurance that joint decisions provided. He hadn't realised how much he had relied on Barbara's support.

His mind turned to the day the pair of them had decided to buy their home. She'd gone through the house, which had obviously been allowed to deteriorate by the previous elderly owner – and pointed out what she would do to each room in turn. He had marvelled at her imagination and become caught up in her enthusiasm. Where he saw peeling wallpaper she saw bright cream emulsion. Where he saw an ancient boiler she saw a new double oven. Then they bought the house and together had transformed it into her ideal. He was happy that she was happy and when Carole was born their lives seemed complete.

Then their daughter grew up and moved away. He lost his job and Barbara seemed to be occupied in ways she did not share with him. He supposed he had just got into a rut. There didn't seem to be anything in his life that he wanted to share with anyone. Adverts on the TV and radio irritated him. He found himself shouting at people who appeared to ignore him, especially when he was driving. The weekly shop became an ordeal until, tired of watching other people fussing about, he opted to stay in the car and wait for Barbara to bring the shopping for him to pack in the boot.

He stared at the dates on the nearest gravestone. Only forty years between birth and death. That was years ago. How long was the average now? He should have another twenty years at least. What was he going to do with that time?

There was no escaping the fact that he needed more than fishing and football to make the move to the coast. He couldn't risk changing his life until he had the offer of a job. Without another person in his life he had to feel needed. He would return home – get rid of all traces of Barbara and make a real effort to find a job near his new friends.

He stood up, full of resolve, and realised he wasn't certain which way to go. He'd come at the cemetery from the right, hadn't he? Was he moving uphill or down?

Could he see a spire or other landmark he recognised? He listened for traffic. If he found a main road he would probably know where he was. He felt the stirrings of hunger. If he saw a pub he would stop for a bite to eat. After all, there was nothing to rush back for, was there? Nothing was going to be settled in a hurry.

He reached a railway bridge and, walking under it, recognised where he was. A transport café provided him with an all day breakfast and a mug of tea. Satisfied, he made his way home and found a note from the estate agent.

'Please ring on return,' He couldn't be bothered. He'd do it after the weekend. He opened a can of beer and turned on the TV. All his energy would go into finding work. Once that was achieved he might become content.

Tania was back at her pilates class. She was just rolling up her mat when she was approached by two of the other women.

"It's Pat's birthday on Saturday and we're all going to the Italian for lunch. Would you like to come?"

Pat was the instructor and someone Tania would really like to know better. "I'll try," she said.

"Well, we're meeting at twelve o'clock. I'll put you down as long as you give me a ring if you can't make it," and she reeled off her mobile number.

All the way home on the bus Tania agonised over how to talk to Ellen. Should she ask her, or tell her? Should she assume she had permission to go or treat it like a favour? What was she, a woman or a mouse? By the time she reached number 24 she still hadn't made up her mind.

As usual, Ellen wanted to know all about her afternoon and it seemed natural to tell her about the birthday lunch.

"I suppose you'd like to attend?" said Ellen , haughtily.

"If it's not inconvenient." Tania felt herself dropping into submissive mode.

"As long as it doesn't become a habit."

There was a note in Ellen's voice that Tania hadn't noticed recently. 'Imperious,' was a word that sprang to mind. Ellen had been softer, more like a friend than an employer and Tania had begun to like her, but now she was feeling uncomfortable in her presence. The two women said little to each other that evening and Tania went to bed feeling unsettled and disturbed.

Hadn't secrets been part of the problem between her and her husband? Now it seemed the pattern was being repeated. She needed an occasion like Saturday to restore her sanity.

For the next few days Tania was surprised to find Ellen spending most of her time upstairs. Tania sat in the lounge trying to read but wondering all the time what she was doing. Mealtimes were superficially normal but conversation was difficult. Tania felt that Ellen's mind was elsewhere and wondered if she was regretting accepting Tania as a companion.

When Saturday came and Ellen had not appeared at breakfast time, Tania went to the bottom of the stairs and called up. "Ellen, I'm off now. Can I bring you anything?"

Ellen's door opened and she responded, "No thank you. Have a nice time."

Perhaps, thought Tania, things would get back to normal when she returned.

The other women greeted her warmly and made an effort to include her in their chatter but much of it was about holidays or television programmes and she could contribute little to the conversation

Her carbonara was delicious – but, with garlic bread, more than she could manage at lunchtime and she blushed when the waiter asked if he could remove her plate. She declined a dessert.

Finally, from one of the younger members, came the question she had been dreading. "Have you any children, Tania?"

Hoping it was not a mistake, she replied. "Yes, one daughter – but she lives up north."

"My Josie is at college in Manchester. She's studying Art History. Goodness only knows what use that will be," and the conversation moved on to a discussion on how difficult it was for graduates to find employment.

Tania excused herself after coffee and retreated to the promenade. It didn't seem to matter whether the tide was way out or right in, she still loved being by the sea.

She tried ringing Carole but there was no signal. She hadn't called back and Tania tried not to feel disappointed. She'd wanted to be a new person, hadn't she? Well she had what she wanted and that meant leaving the old life behind.

A couple of boys sped round her on skates and she stepped onto the cobbles to avoid them. Couples were strolling hand in hand;there were buggies, wheelchairs and people with dogs on leads.

Everyone looked either happy or at peace – perhaps the seaside does that to you – she thought. She should come down here more often. But she knew Ellen would be expecting her back so she made her way past the hospital to Cavendish Road.

She let herself in and looked for Ellen in the downstairs rooms but she wasn't there. When she entered the kitchen she found the back door ajar and she could just see Ellen bending over something further down the garden, near the hedge. She looked as if she was digging!

Tania couldn't believe her eyes. Ellen – digging in the garden! She had shown no interest in planting anything – besides, it was too early to be putting in plants.

Ellen paused, leaning on the spade, holding her back. Should Tania go out and help?

She had the impression that Ellen was doing this while Tania was out so that she could keep it a secret. Another secret!

Tania turned away from the window and went upstairs. She would be able to see Ellen from her bedroom and maybe find out why she had been digging.

By the time she reached her room Ellen had completed her task and was wheeling a barrow back to the garden shed. The only way Tania was going to find out what she had buried was to ask her. She certainly didn't relish the thought of trying to dig it up – whatever it was. Should she go down and confront her – or try to bring it up when she could judge her companion's mood?

She decided to wait until they had dinner. She would give Ellen time to leave the kitchen and then go down and start preparing the meal – quiche lorraine with peas and potato croquettes, followed by chocolate mousse, Ellen's favourite. She was trying hard to make up for being absent all day.

"You look tired, Ellen," she said when they'd finished their dessert. "Would you like coffee now, or later?"

"Later, please, dear. Tell me about your party."

"It wasn't really a party – just a lunch. I gave Pat the ankle warmers I'd bought and she seemed pleased."

"What did you have to eat?"

"Carbonara and garlic bread. It was very nice."

"Were there any menfolk there?"

"No, only girls. Then I went to look at the sea. You should go down there more often, Ellen, it's invigorating."

"I don't think I need invigorating. I need renewing. Let's go sit in the lounge. You can read to me, something soothing – and don't be disappointed if I fall asleep."

Tania held her arm while they moved slowly into the front room. Ellen sighed softly as she eased herself into the large armchair.

Looking along the shelves Tania asked, "How about Kipling – you've heard the Just So Stories so many times it won't matter if you miss a bit?"

"Lovely, dear," and the old lady stifled a yawn.

I've missed my opportunity, thought Tania. How can I ask her what she was digging for?

She opened the book and began reading but she had hardly reached the third page when she noticed tears running down her listener's face.

"Not that story, love. Not today, please."

"What is it? What's happened?"

"She died. She died almost as soon as he was born."

"Who died?"

"Sheba, my dog."

"You had a dog?"

"Yes. She was pregnant. I kept her upstairs. She had one puppy, but something went wrong. The puppy survived, but she didn't."

"And you've buried her in the garden."

"Yes. How did you know?"

"I saw you. What happened to the puppy?"

"He's upstairs. I'm glad I've told you because now I can bring him down in the warm. He's very weak."

"He needs his mother's milk. We'll have to feed him – or find another bitch to do it. I'll ring the Animal Ambulance." Tania put down the book and stood, waiting for instructions.

"I didn't think of that. I was so upset about Sheba."

"Can I see the puppy? What have you called him?"

"I haven't thought. He's black, not like his mother. She was a kind of husky."

"Why didn't you tell me you had a dog?"

Ellen seemed to shrink at the question and looked away as she replied."It's personal. I don't think you would understand."

Tania felt hurt by the remark but did not press the matter. She was afraid Ellen might close up altogether and she hoped finding the puppy might lead to further revelations.

"I'll fetch him down," said Ellen abruptly, "But once the vet has seen him and he's been weaned I'll want him back."

"Of course."Tania followed her out into the corridor and turned towards the hall table.

Flipping through the local telephone book she found the number. Once she'd explained the situation they confirmed they would be with them that evening.

Ellen came downstairs with the puppy in a dog basket. It was giving tiny cries and it looked limp. It was almost black, with hints of grey and brown and three white paws.

"I think I'd like to call him Lupus," said Ellen as she entered the kitchen. "What do you think?"

"That's an interesting choice," replied Tania not daring to contradict her companion.

They soaked a rag in warm water and held it out for the puppy to suck – but it just whimpered and moved its head away. They waited impatiently until there was a knock on the front door.

It was a relief to hand Lupus over to the people in the animal ambulance who reassured the two women that they would soon find a nursing bitch and had no doubts about the puppy's welfare.

Tania was left wondering about the dog who had sired Lupus. She had the feeling it could have been Fiona's black labrador, Monty. She resolved to explore the garden the next day and see if she could find any gaps in the fence. She'd never been down to the far end and was hopeful, now that Spring was on the way, she could spend some time outside.

That night Tania dreamed she was back at work – putting someone's hair in rollers, but when she looked up at the mirror she saw her husband. He was in a garden, digging a hole – a long, coffin-shaped hole, and he was shouting, "Shut up, shut up!" each time he struck the soil with his spade.

Then the scene changed and they were eating breakfast. He was piling three spoonfuls of sugar into his tea.

She heard her own voice saying, "You don't need all that sugar. You aren't using as much energy as you used to," and she saw his face crumple into a scowl.

His fingers tightened round the mug and he grunted with rage as he hurled it at her. It smashed against the fridge, sending shards of pottery across the floor, while the contents splashed onto her arms and down her bare legs, not burning, but hot enough to be alarming.

She got up and tried to run for the door – but her legs felt heavy and would not move quickly. She was crying with frustration when she woke and opened her eyes to the peace and darkness of her bedroom.

What had made her remember? Did seeing Ellen with a spade make her think that it could be used as a weapon as well as a tool? Did she subconsciously think she deserved to be punished for not understanding her husband's problems? Was she worried that he would rather bury her than know she could live her life without him? How much should she fear that he would find her? Was she making him out to be a bigger monster than he really was to justify her own actions?

She turned over and tried to sleep, but morning came before she could get the disturbing images out of her mind.

Nine

Tony was pleased with the CV he had written and sent out. He had two promising referees and a glowing report from his previous boss. It was only his age that might be seen as a disadvantage, but his experience should make him a better bet than a youngster, or someone from abroad.

While one company ignored his approach, two others said they were sorry they were not recruiting and one asked him to go for an interview. They were the smallest of the four companies he had applied to – and he didn't know which routes they had. He determined to go back down to Brighton early and investigate.

He drove down the day before the interview and enquired among his friends but only one could give him any information.

"They don't cover Brighton," he said. "They've got a fleet of old bangers and they do school runs and fill in routes that the big boys don't cover. It will be all pensioners and kids."

"I don't mind that," replied Tony. "As long as I can have a full time job I'll be happy."

"It'll be full time all right. You'll have to be part driver, part mechanic. Good luck to you."

Tony drove over to the industrial estate where the bus garage was sited. He was early and sat in the car watching the building. Only one bus left the depot while he was there, an elderly green bone-shaker which made him smile.

Finally, a reasonable ten minutes before he was due, he strolled over and opened the door to the office.

It was warm, but bare, with a bench along two walls and a partition at the far end. The walls were covered with maps, charts and timetables. There was one poster of a vintage coach driving up a winding road between two vivid green hills.

Before he had time to take in any more of his surroundings a door in the partition opened and a short man with a round shiny face called him in. He didn't introduce himself but Tony assumed he was the manager. The man took his place behind a desk and invited Tony to sit. Before him he had a pile of papers and two telephones.

"Now, Mr Sharp. This all looks very impressive. What makes you want to move to this area?"

"I'm downsizing, as the house I am in now is too big for a single man. My wife and daughter live elsewhere." (He wasn't lying – just giving an inaccurate impression.)

"Do you have somewhere to live in this area?"

"Not yet. I have an eye on a residential mobile home but I need to sell my house first."

"How long do you think that will take? We need someone fairly urgently."

"That wouldn't be a problem. I have friends who will put me up in the meantime. I'd like to get back to work as soon as possible."

"Not all our vehicles are new. How are you on maintenance?"

"Pretty good. I do all the work on my own car."

"We'd like to give you a trial. Learning the routes takes a while so we put all new drivers on as observers for a couple of weeks, on full pay. I'd need to see all your up to date documentation. We have company insurance but I need sight of yours to ensure you have no medical problems that might affect the cover. Welcome to RR Coaches."

"RR?"

"Rural Routes, but it hints at Rest and Recreation. Would you like a cup of tea? I'll take you over to the workshop and introduce you to whoever's there. If you could start before the end of March we'd be grateful. I'll give you some more information before you go – Health and Safety, standard pay rates, hours etc. Give me a ring if there's anything you don't understand."

He stood and ushered Tony out of the office and round to the back of the building. Two rusty buses stood next to a large garage and from the rear of the building came the sound of metal on metal.

"Good, someone's there," said the manager. "Come and get acquainted."

Tony drove back to Brighton feeling happier than he had for months. Somebody actually wanted to employ him. He'd even been exonerated over the car accident. It seems the car in front and the one behind were at fault for sandwiching him. His luck had changed and he felt like celebrating.

Fortunately his friends were quite content to join him and he ended the evening singing sea shanties and falling up the stairs to bed in a drunken stupor.

He woke the next morning, lying on the bed, still in his clothes, with only his boots removed, and a head like a jack hammer. He took off his trousers and crawled under the covers and then realised he was desperately thirsty. Once up, he splashed his face and, fully dressed, went in search for some coffee.

He couldn't go on staying at the hotel. He had to make sure the sale of his house went through and visit the mobile home site to see if he could bare to live in such a tiny space.

He rang the owner and asked if the home was still on the market.

"Yes – were you interested?"

"I'd like to have a look at it. Would today be convenient?"

"As soon as you like. I'm here all day."

"Fine. I'll be with you at eleven."

Maybe the voice had been somewhat abrupt but that's what men were like. It was good to deal with someone who just wanted to get down to business without any shillyshallying.

The van (he couldn't quite think of it as a home yet) was more spacious than he had expected. It wasn't new, of course, but it had all the necessary furniture and equipment, except a TV and beds. He didn't mind the décor – a kind of bluey-grey, and could easily bring a small table so that he could eat in the large room while watching television. There was some rust around the windows and he would have preferred blinds to the patterned curtains but the kitchen was even better equipped than his kitchen in Kent.

The best thing about the place was the added porch. The substantial wooden and glass lean to would be perfect for his fishing gear as long as it was secure. He wouldn't let on straight away, but this made the whole thing more acceptable.

"Two bedrooms isn't much," he grumbled to the owner. "That second one isn't very big."

"But there's only one of you, isn't there? Or are you planning to bring lots of visitors?"

Was he hinting at something? Tony felt wary. Had he made the wrong impression?

"No. I'm all on my own. It's just difficult to think of moving from a full sized house to one of these."

The man seemed satisfied with the reply and when Tony told him about his new job his manner thawed.

"There's damp in that top corner," Tony complained.

"Well, it's a few years old. A new one would cost you twice the price."

"I'll need a night to think about it."

"There's others interested."

"I'll let you know tomorrow morning. How about a £300 reduction?"

"£100. I can't go lower."

"And the site fees?"

"Everything else is in the office. I'll show you now."

Tony had no intention of leaving without making a purchase and when everything else seemed satisfactory he left a deposit and returned to Brighton. Now he had both a job and a new home. The estate agent had confirmed that the sale of his house was going ahead. He would soon have a base on the coast and money to spare.

Lupus the puppy was back with Ellen and Tania by the beginning of April and Tania could hardly believe the difference it made to her companion. Firstly she asked Tania to go shopping with her for some new clothes. They bought stout lace up shoes and wide leg trousers.

Ellen looked at herself in the store mirror and laughed. "It's years since I wore slacks. I just wish I felt as fit as I look."

The two of them walked the little dog in the park and bought toys that squeaked and balls that rolled for him to play with.

Then Tania found Ellen trying to train the dog to sit and stay and realised that, once more, she was taking on the role of commander. When the puppy responded well he was rewarded with treats but when he grew bored and did not react as required Ellen grew angry – she hissed, rather than shouted, and shut the little creature in the the garden shed until she calmed down and let him out.

Yet however badly she treated him, Lupus seemed to adore her and would sit by her feet at night and wag his tail whenever she spoke.

Tania waited until the next sunny day and ventured out into the garden. Much of the fence near the railway was obscured by brambles and unkempt hedging but she did find a couple of places where a fox or dog could push through. She blocked them off as best she could with bricks and wood that was lying around. The only use for the end of the garden appeared to be a large compost heap. The section leading onto the railway was part wood and part wire, then a bank of buddlia bushes before the lines themselves.

Satisfied that the puppy couldn't get through, she returned back towards the house. Looking to one side she saw something she hadn't noticed before. It was a pond, or it had been a pond. It was dry now but the curious thing about it was the little stone animals arranged around the edges. There was a bird, tipping forward as if it was about to drink, and a squirrel, sat on its hind legs chewing a nut. Next to it was a rabbit, turning away from the pool, as if it was about to flee, and beyond the pond was the remains of a Wendy House, the colour faded and the wood flaking and rotten, with no glass in the windows, a forlorn and neglected sight. Tania had seen no other sign of a child in the house but she realised, then, that Ellen must have spent her formative years playing in this garden.

She had disappeared upstairs, to lord it over the mannequins in the strange room, she supposed. She wondered what Lupus thought of his mistress's odd habits.

Maybe this was the opportunity she had been waiting for to find out for herself how peculiar Ellen really was.

She took off her muddy shoes and tiptoed up the stairs.

Without the fur coats she could never have remained hidden but when she tried the door handle of the room it turned easily and she stepped inside.

Gently she parted the furs, and, as she did so, she could hear Ellen's voice declaiming loudly.

Was she spouting poetry?

Tania bent forward to get a better view and her eyes were drawn to the tall, upright figure at the head of the table. It was Ellen, but Ellen in costume. On her head she had a long dark wig, held in place with a gold band.

Her body was clad in a fur tunic, with a rust red cloak across her shoulders and what looked like a long leather skirt. She had a gold chain round her neck and various coloured amulets.

> *"Bid him repair to me and bring with him*
> *some of the chiefest princes of the Goths*
>
> *Bid him encamp his soldiers where they are.*
>
> *Tell him the Emperor and the Empress too*
>
> *Feast at my house – and he shall*
> *feast with them."* [1]

With these words she flung the cloak back over her shoulder and raised her chin in an attitude of dominance.

Tania couldn't help herself. She tried to stifle a giggle but the coat wobbled on the hanger and the sound must have alerted Ellen to her audience.

"Who's there?" she called out. "Lupus, see who's there!"

The puppy, who had been under the table at his mistress's feet, jumped up with a delighted bark and

---

[1] Titus Andronicus. Act 5. Scene 1.

bounded towards Tania.

She just had time to wriggle through the door and close it before she was discovered. She fled down the stairs, afraid of what might happen next.

It must have taken Ellen a few seconds to reach the door and let Lupus out. He reached Tania just as she got to the lowest step and, turning, she tried to look unconcerned as she looked up.

"Did you call, Ellen?" she asked, as calmly as she could.

The puppy was dancing round her feet and Ellen shrank back into the shadows.

"No, dear. I was just playing with Lupus," she muttered and moved quickly out of sight.

That evening, after dinner, Ellen didn't ask for a game. Instead, she began to talk about her days in the theatre.

"I could have been a classical actress, you know," she said. "But each time I auditioned there was someone better known than I was who got the part. There was something about the wicked queen characters that drew me to them.

My grandmother was a gypsy, you know, and a medium. She said there would one day be royalty in this house. Well, it hasn't happened yet – unless you count all the different monarchs I have played in my time. I used to feel I had some special power and that Sheba was my connection with the spirit world.

Lupus isn't the same. He is too much of this earth. He isn't tuned in to me as Sheba was. Only time will tell if he can help me achieve my destiny."

What destiny? thought Tania. Was she deluding herself that she was somehow special? It would explain why she put on such airs and graces – but she'd shown no sign of wanting to perform magic.

"They should be stone," muttered Ellen. "Then I would know I had inherited my grandmother's powers."

Her eyes had taken on a strange gleam and her fingers clawed the air as if she was reaching for an invisible wand.

Tania didn't know whether to interrupt her or let her carry on in that trance-like state, but Ellen's head dropped onto her chest and a long shudder went through her body. When she lifted her face Tania could see nothing but the usual haughty stare. Then Ellen smiled, a thin, secret kind of smile.

"If I was in the forest I would have the power to make them into stone. You'll help me, won't you?"

"I'll do what I can, Ellen."

"It is all that needs to happen to show I have succeeded."

Tania didn't know how to reply. Did Ellen know she had seen inside the secret room? Did she expect the mannequins to turn to stone? Did she really think she was a witch?

"I think it's time we called it a day," she said, trying to bring her companion back to reality. "Sleep will make everything clearer."

Ellen's face lost its fanatical gleam. "Yes, sleep will refresh us. You are right," and she turned without a backward glance and left Tania alone in the room.

She's mad, thought Tania, or at least, obsessed. Should she see a doctor about it? Yet until recently she would have said Ellen was reasonably sane. Was it the death of her beloved pet that had unhinged her, or had she always been delusional and managed to hide it from Tania?

She had told Tania that she was the best companion she had ever had and now that trust would be sorely tested. There were only two people she could discuss her worries with, Ted and Fiona. They might have had some inkling of when Ellen started to collect the mannequins. She determined to see them as soon as possible.

The following morning saw Tania seated in her neighbour's kitchen trying to think how to to start to tell them about Ellen. It was made more difficult because Ellen had shown no sign that anything was wrong that day and, in fact, had seemed unusually cheerful. She had sent Tania out to buy some treats for the puppy and some turkish delight and seemed perfectly content to go for her usual appointment to the hairdresser's.

"Has anyone ever said anything about Ellen's grand-mother?" she began, at last.

"The old witch, you mean?" replied Ted. "We didn't see much of her when she lived there. She frightened the local children – always looked as if she belonged in a story book."

"Do you think Ellen takes after her?"

"Not really. Ellen was always dramatic and colourful but not scary. Then, when she retreated into her shell, we just forgot about her."

"Did anything happen to cause that?"

"The death of her parents, I suppose. For a while she had theatrical types visiting – especially the lady who made costumes – but gradually that tailed off and she stopped going out."

"I've seen her out with you and the puppy," said Fiona.

"Yes, and it looks a bit like Monty, doesn't it?" Tania laughed.

"It could have been..." Fiona paused. "He has been keen to get out, but we've had him seen to now – so it shouldn't happen again."

"It doesn't matter. Ellen loves the little beast. It's just that she's been acting rather strangely."

"Just humour her," said Ted. "She lives in a bit of a dream world, I expect."

"Maybe. I hope that's all it is. I don't know what I'd do if she really went peculiar."

"I think you've been good for her, Tania. You may have stopped her going over the edge."

"Thanks for saying that, Ted. We were getting on so well until recently. Perhaps it's just a phase. I did hope we were developing an understanding."

It was a much happier Tania who walked back to number 24.

As she did so a large black car drove away from the front of the house. It looked as though Ellen had had a visitor, but she'd said nothing about it to Tania.

She opened the door quickly and looked into the lounge. There was no sign of Ellen but the bureau flap was open. She was about to close it when Ellen and Lupus came in from the hall. Ellen was dressed in a smart powder blue woollen suit and her hair was pinned up, showing her lean features but giving her an air of extreme elegance.

"Ah, you're back. I'll do that," she said, briskly and closed the bureau.

"You look smart," Tania couldn't help remarking.

"It's good to have a change," Ellen replied, enigmatically. "How about a cup of tea?"

If Tania had thought that having tea together would lead to an admission she was mistaken. Ellen seemed on edge – nervous energy making her spill the sugar and frighten Lupus.

"Sit still, Lupus," she commanded and the dog sat obediently watching as she broke a biscuit in half and gave him some.

"I think Monty from along the road might have been Lupus' father," Tania began.

"I wouldn't be surprised. It doesn't matter. It's the maternal line that's important."

Important for what? Thought Tania – but she needed to get away from her companion. Ellen was so fidgety it was making her uncomfortable. "I must get changed," she said and almost ran out of the door and up the stairs.

It was only when she was alone that she began to piece together what she knew about Ellen's delusions. Her grandmother had behaved like a witch. Ellen the actress, had enjoyed playing witches. She used to have a wolf-like dog. Did she think she was a witch? Did that tableau in the mystery room make her believe she had magic powers? If so, what kind of a witch did she think she was?

Then it dawned on her. Ellen wanted to be the witch in the children's story – the white queen who hated Christmas and gave the boy turkish delight. She was the queen who turned things to stone! Ellen's fantasies were based on a story book!

At first the mannequins must have satisfied her. She could use her imagination to pretend they were stone – but the death of her dog Sheba, whom she had invested with magical powers – had made her face reality and her dream had been shattered. As if the thought reflected what was happening there came a loud crash from the floor below. Tania heard a screech, a bang and a series of crunching, ripping sounds.

She ran down the stairs and straight into the mystery room. It wasn't difficult to get inside, most of the coats were off their hangers and strewn about the floor. The room was almost completely destroyed.

The mannequins were in pieces, heads and limbs rolling about the floor or flung over broken chairs. All that remained whole was the long table which Ellen was hammering furiously with a dismembered arm. As Tania watched she ripped away the sleeve and brought the hand down on the table with a vicious thump.

Her white hair was loose and flapping across her eyes. Her once pale face was red with exertion and her shrill voice filled the room. "You dare to disobey me," she shrieked. "You owe your existence to me – and this is how you repay me. Never, never will you cross me again! I don't need you," she shrieked and flung the arm across the room.

Then, seeing Tania, she froze. She looked round in panic for an excuse for her behaviour and, finding none, collapsed ,breathless, onto the throne. Her head dropped and she began to cry – loud, hysterical sobs. "I'm sorry," she gulped. "I couldn't bear it any longer. I don't know what's happening to me."

Tania was overcome with pity for the old lady. It looked as if all her dreams had been destroyed in one brief session. She didn't know how important the room had been to Ellen but she suspected that the loss of that outlet might prove disastrous to her companion. Had the models been alive she may have been satisfied with applause, had they been stone she could have believed she had magic powers, but when she recognised that they were plastic it must have sent her into a paroxysm of despair. The line between what she wanted to be and the reality of her life had been breached. Without her 'wolf' she could no longer pretend to herself that she was the White Witch.

Without this alternative persona she was just an ageing actress with nothing but memories, no family, no power, no future. The reality of the situation could have been enough to drive her insane.

"You didn't need them," she soothed. "You've got me – and Lupus. You don't need more. We love you," and in saying the words she realised that they were true. She really had come to love the old lady and was concerned that this was a breakdown that might need more help than she could provide.

Ellen was shaking. "I'm cold," she murmured. "Awfully cold."

"I know," said Tania. "You go to your room now. I'll bring you a hot water bottle. You need a rest. You aren't hurt, are you?"

"I don't think so." Ellen's teeth were chattering.

"You've had a shock. You must get warm. I'll help you get to bed. It's all over now."

"Thank you, dear. You are a treasure. I told Mr Trentham," and she let Tania lead her back to her bedroom.

Once the hot water bottle was provided and Tania had brushed the tangled strands of hair away from her face, Ellen sat back on the pillow and closed her eyes. Tania waited until she was sure she was sleeping and then went looking for Lupus.

The poor dog was cowering under the big table in the other room.

Tania thought about trying to tidy it but changed her mind. She would leave that until later and take Lupus out while it was still light. They both needed to be out of the house for a short while. When she returned perhaps she would be able to make sense of it all.

Ten

riving home to Kent, Tony's good mood soon evaporated. "Wait, you stupid bastard," he shouted as an elderly man looked as if he was going to pull out of his drive as Tony drove past.

He didn't want to go home. He didn't want the hassle of packing up and he certainly didn't want the job of selecting what to take and what to leave behind.

He couldn't ask Carole to come and help – she'd be preparing for the new baby. The more he thought about it the more he resented the fact that his wife had left him. It wasn't enough that he could forge a new life for himself – he wanted to punish her, and to do that he must find her. Then he laughed out loud. Of course, in his new job he was almost sure to see her. True – the company he was joining was not the one of the bus he believed she used but if she still didn't drive she might still use the same bus stops.

Everything pointed to fate taking a hand to help him. All he had to do was complete the sale of his old house. He would tell the prospective buyers that all the kitchen fittings and furniture could be part of the sale for a nominal sum. He'd have the greatest pleasure in throwing out everything that had belonged to Barbara. If she wasn't coming back he'd make sure there was nothing to come back to!

Carole had one more week at work and then she was taking maternity leave.

She'd met a couple of other mums-to-be and they had instigated a rota so that each week they met in one another's houses to compare notes and once she'd finished work they had invited her to join them.

"If we all have our babies about the same time we can go to the mother and baby club at the church hall," said Jill.

"I'm sure to be late," responded Maria. "I hope I am because I haven't bought half the things you are supposed to buy."

"Don't take any notice of those magazines," said Jill. "Those ladies in London must be made of money, look at this – pram, cot ,car seat, moses basket, bedding bale, sleeping bag,carrycot,nappies and clothes galore! My baby will have seven babygro's and like it!"

"But you know it's a boy,"said Carole. "I told them I didn't want to know."

"So did I," said Maria, "but Jill's already got a girl – she had an excuse."

"I'm not sure having a boy and a girl is so great," said Jill, "Maybe if they were the same sex they'd get on better."

"You get what you're given," said Maria. "As long as

they're healthy. What do you want, Carole?"

"I think I'd prefer a girl. Boys seem to grow away from their mothers as they get older and without a role model..."

"I'm sorry. I didn't think – but you might find yourself another man."

"When I've got a child? I doubt it." There was a wistfulness in her reply. It would be nice, she thought, if she could find another partner but she would have baggage. Where would she find a man willing to take on someone else's child? One thing for sure, if she had a girl she would make sure she never abandoned her. Pride had stopped her from calling her mother back. The situation was just too complicated to address over the phone, but maybe it was time she tried. No, she'd wait until after the birth. She wanted to have good news to tell her.

That evening she had a call from her father.

"I've sold the house," he said, "I've got a box full of your old stuff. I'm taking it down to the coast. I've bought a mobile home. It's got two bedrooms and I'll fit one out for you and the infant so you can visit. Is there anything you need?"

"Not really. It would be nice if you could come up and see the house before baby is born. I'm sorry Mum isn't around."

"Stuff her. I can drive up next weekend if you like. I'm starting a new job soon but there's nothing needing doing down there yet. These park homes have everything in them already. I'll bring you some pictures."

Carole smiled. Her father sounded much more like his old self. Maybe her mother leaving had been good for him after all. She would have to give him her bedroom and sleep in the baby's room on a Z bed. He was very set in his ways and she wondered what he would think of her little northern town.

Tony was tired. It was a long way to drive alone and his one stop angered him because of the price of everything in the service station. If Barbara had been with him she would have chosen the stopping places carefully so that he could have a break. She would have packed a picnic so they didn't have to pay extortionate prices.

By the time he reached Carole's he was too exhausted to do anything other than swallow a bowlful of soup,eat three slices of buttered toast and finish the whole lot off with a tot of whisky.

There was nowhere to leave the car except in the narrow road in front of the terrace and he went to bed hoping it would be safe.

Next morning Tony began to wonder why he had come. Having breakfast with a pregnant young woman, even if it was his own daughter -seemed so unnatural. He couldn't feel enthusiastic about the birth. It just seemed to add to life's complications.

If there had been another man around he could have swapped stories and sympathised with his situation but Carole made him feel old and out of touch. She always had got on better with her mother.

"You should get a computer, Dad," she said, "Then we could chat on Skype."

"Maybe – when I'm in the new place," he said, unconvincingly.

He did his best to shift furniture and load up the freezer but after two days of finding they had little to talk about he took his leave. Carole had given the impression that she had everything under control and he envied her her confidence.

Still, the new job awaited, the sale of his old house was going through and he'd have plenty of savings left after buying the mobile home. It was a pity he had to leave so much behind but perhaps it was better that way. He was making a new start.

Carole's head was swimming. She was overwhelmed by a sense of inadequacy. She'd kept up the pretence of efficiency in front of her father but now she didn't know whether to buy books, look on the internet or ask the midwives. Each time she thought she had everything planned and ready she thought of something else she ought to do.

Should she buy a cot or rely on the moses basket? Should she use ordinary bedding or buy a sleeping bag? What kind of pram and car seat did she need? What about a baby monitor?

She alternated between feeling confident that she could cope alone and anger that neither the baby's father nor her own mother were there to share this with her.

She couldn't believe how she could have been fooled into thinking that Paul really cared for her enough to leave his family, and she felt especially hurt that her mother had disappeared without telling her where she was going. She resisted the temptation to try the number Barbara had given her. The more she thought about her the more resentment she felt.

In a way she hoped the baby would be a girl, but she'd kept to the tradition of not knowing the sex before the birth. She'd chosen Gary Jason as a name for a boy and if it was a girl, Lucy April. That's if she comes in April, thought Carole. Otherwise she'll be Lucy May.

Then it snowed. Carole was glad she had a fridge freezer with enough food to last her over a few days but she still ran out of milk and had to dig her way out of the front door to get to the nearest shop. Many people had shovelled the snow away from their doors but occasionally she had to hold onto the wall of the houses to stop herself slipping on the icy pavement.

She felt clumsy and awkward as she stamped the snow off her boots and pushed open the door to the little newsagents'. The bell rang and the warmth felt steamy and welcoming as she struggled to stay upright and remember what she needed.

"Sit down, hon. Get your breath. There's no rush," said the woman behind the counter.

"Thanks, I will," responded Carole. "I didn't realise how strong the wind was."

She looked around the tiny shop. There was a section for food and necessities as well as the counter with sweets and papers. She'd been in before – but usually just to pay her paper bill. Most of her food purchases had been from the supermarket.

Two large refrigerators were at the back of the shop with butter, yoghurt and milk as well as the usual frozen food. Carole felt the baby kick as she rose and waddled past the cereals and biscuits and collected a 2pint carton of milk. Then she scoured the shelves for some tinned milk in case she got snowed in and added a loaf of bread, some chocolate biscuits and a tin of peas. With a couple of bananas that seemed to be enough to carry, even if it was only a few yards back to her house.

By the time she reached home she was tense with exertion and collapsed on a chair for a rest before unpacking her shopping. Then she made a cup of tea and opened the packet of biscuits.

"I don't know about having a baby," she said to the bump, "I feel like a baby myself sometimes," and she laughed ruefully.

Tania was becoming concerned about Ellen. Since her outburst against the mannequins she had gone very quiet and would not venture out of her bedroom. She seemed afraid to tackle the stairs.

Tania tidied the room she now thought of as the theatre and disposed of all the remnants of the models and chairs.

The tall throne remained at the head of the table but she had not been able to save many of the platters. Even the backcloth of the stone castle had been shattered in the rumpus and Tania discovered a tiny space where Ellen had kept Sheba and her puppy.

It was a sad and lonely room and Tania wished she could bring some life back into it.

The fur coats were now with the other costumes in the dressing room and the big empty room,with its wooden floor, would make an ideal studio or playroom, she thought.

It was no good dreaming about such possibilities when she had a sick woman on her hands – for Ellen alternated bouts of lucidity with hysterical rages and violent weeping. Then, exhausted, she would sleep for hours – only to wake in the middle of the night and call out for Tania.

Tania's life became one round of soothing, feeding, washing and reading. She began to lose all sense of day or night.

When she called the doctor out all he could offer was a place in a nursing home for Ellen but she wouldn't leave her house. Eventually Tania paid for two hours a week with a carer so that she could get some time to herself.

Ellen was getting fussier and fussier about her meals and Tania could only watch while she grew thinner and weaker.

It was when she refused her favourite banana sandwich, with the crusts removed, that Tania finally lost her temper. "Right – tell me what you DO want!" she shouted. "Because I can't think how else to help you."

Ellen burst into tears. "I don't know. I can't help it. I don't remember." she spluttered.

"Oh, I'm sorry. Would you like some milk and honey? I must be tired."

"What a good idea. I used to love that as a child." Ellen's face took on the wistful air of someone remembering happier days.

It was a relief to get out of the room and into the kitchen but Tania felt like crying herself. She wasn't trained for this. True – she'd looked after her mother before she died but she had been resigned to her fate. Her pain had been alleviated by pills. The only pills Ellen was given sent her to sleep – and when she woke she was more disorientated than ever.

When Tania went upstairs with the warm drink, Lupus was curled up on the bed beside his mistress and Ellen was stroking him absent-mindedly.

"I'll sit you up a bit, shall I?" said Tania.

"Yes, all right , dear – but don't move the dog."

However, as soon as Ellen shifted, the dog jumped down and went to the bedroom door to be let out.

"Don't fret, Ellen," said Tania. "I'll let him into the garden and bring him straight back."

It was when Carole was washing up her breakfast things that she suddenly felt a dampness between her legs. Then there was a sudden whoosh as her waters broke.

That's peculiar, she thought. She hadn't had any contractions. It was a week before the due date but she had a bag packed for the hospital.

Trying not to panic, she rang the hospital and told them what had happened.

The reassuring voice at the other end of the phone told her to make her way to the hospital if she could, but not to expect anything else to happen quickly.

Carole found some pads and two pairs of knickers and decided she was fit enough to drive herself the short distance to the hospital.

However, once there, she was told in no uncertain terms that she should have had someone with her. "I don't have anyone,"she confessed. "I haven't lived here very long."

"Well, you'll have to go back home. It's too soon to have you in." said the nurse after she had checked that everything was normal. "You must try to find someone to bring you back when the time comes."

Carole felt chastened by the reprimand. Why hadn't she thought of someone? The other women had talked about their 'birth partners' but Carole had shut her ears to the discussions about whether husbands or mothers were best.

She felt like an idiot but the only woman she had chatted to outside work was Mrs Bennet in the local shop. She was nice and near – but Carole didn't even know if she could drive.

She parked the car behind the house and made her way to the newsagents.'

Mr and Mrs Bennet lived above the shop and Mr Bennet had a van – but they worked very long hours and she almost turned back.

The warmth and light in the shop always made her feel welcome and as she waited for Mrs Bennet to finish serving a customer she tried to think how to phrase her request.

Suddenly a sharp pain made her double up with a gasp. The two women looked round in alarm.

"It's all right," breathed Carole. "I think the baby's on the way."

"Do you want to sit down, hon?" asked Mrs Bennet. "Can we get you anything?"

"I came to ask a favour," said Carole, desperately. "I'll need a lift to the hospital sometime, but I don't know when."

"Probably in the middle of the night." said the customer.

"You only live a few doors down, don't you, hon?" said Mrs Bennet.

"Yes, and I think you have my telephone number but I don't know yours. It's an imposition, I know – but I'm on my own."

"Don't you fret, hinny. George or I will take you whatever time it is. Just give us a ring and we'll be there. We'll be glad to help. I was there for our Alice so I know what to expect."

"Thank you. Thank you so much." She held onto the door frame as she struggled out of the shop. I must look a wreck, she thought. When I get back I'll wash my hair. I don't feel safe enough to have a bath. She rubbed her stomach, "Well, baby, we'll be seeing each other soon. I just hope I can be a good mother to you."

Eleven

Tony had completed his two weeks observing the other drivers and had been given a figure of eight route that took him out of town to a supermarket and back to the town centre.

As expected, most of the passengers were pensioners and he took very little cash. It was only when a young man got on with two children he had to try to remember what to charge for their fares.

He couldn't get used to the way the passengers said, "Thank you, driver," as they got off and soon he found one or two of them had discovered his first name and he was greeted with "Hallo, Tony," as they boarded. They must have asked the other drivers, he thought. Next thing they'll be asking me about my family, or my holiday plans!

Each time he stopped in the town centre he looked out for Barbara but there was no sign. Perhaps she's moved on, he thought, and found himself wondering if it was time to find another woman to warm his bed.

He didn't enjoy making his own meals and sleeping alone – but what woman was going to take up with him at his age, and where would he find her?

There was a pub not far from the park home site and he began to eat there at least three times a week. After a month he ventured to ask about a darts team and became a reserve player. Working shifts meant he couldn't attend every week but when the others found out how skilled he was, they accepted him willingly.

There was a monthly folk night and although it wasn't Tony's favourite music – he preferred Country and Western – he decided there might be a chance of meeting a friendly female so he began to attend.

He wasn't one for joining in. That had been Barbara's forte, but he did appreciate a good guitar player and enjoyed the occasional entertainer who played a mean fiddle.

It was when an Irish group were playing one Thursday that he met Clodah.

He noticed her because she was dressed in a long green skirt and a brown fringed top and was sitting huddled in a corner as if she wanted to hide from the world. Her long brown curls almost hid her face and made him want to run his fingers through them. He'd always loved long hair and this woman's hair was especially beautiful.

He watched her for almost the entire evening. She bought her own drinks. Two glasses of stout lasted her three hours. When he was sure she didn't have a companion he moved over towards her and asked if he could sit down.

She seemed to shrink away from him but she nodded assent.

At first he pretended he'd only needed to find a table for his beer but, in between songs, he tried to initiate a conversation.

"They're good, aren't they?" he said.

She looked at him with wide brown eyes and answered, "Yes. I try to follow them."

"Do they play somewhere else local?"

"At the Blacksmith's Arms, every Sunday."

"That's out of town?"

"Yes, in Hushington Village."

"I know it. Do you live near there?"

"No." She turned away from him as if she didn't want to continue the conversation.

The band began another song and Tony realised he had discovered as much as he was likely to do for one night. Still, it was a start. He didn't need to get involved with anyone in a hurry. He had his friends in Brighton and he was amazed at how polite the people on the bus were – it was almost like driving the holiday coaches – and that had been a good way to meet new people.

As he grew used to the routes he began to recognise the same faces, and know when someone needed help getting their shopping trolley on and off the bus. He found the firm were more interested in keeping the customers satisfied than sticking strictly to the timetable.

He had every Sunday off, although he was occasionally asked to check over one of the vehicles -and began to go to Brighton for Sunday lunch.

He was establishing a routine, which only interrupted by a telephone call from Carole.

"Dad, the baby's coming early. You don't need to do

anything. I just wanted to tell you I'm going into hospital. I'll be in touch. Don't worry about me. I feel fine."

Tania was worried. Ellen had almost stopped eating and was drinking very little. She rang the doctor, "It's almost as if she's given up," she said, "I don't know what to do."

"I doubt if it will make much difference if we take her into hospital," was the reply. "Have you tried asking her what she would like to happen next?"

"Not in so many words. She's asleep a lot of the time."

"The painkillers will do that. How about a few days in the hospice?"

"That sounds dreadfully final."

"She's never mentioned any relatives. Do you know if she has any?"

"No. The only person she keeps muttering about is her grandmother."

"I'll send the nurse round to give you a break. You sound exhausted."

"I am. I don't know what I'll do if the worst happens."

"She is over 80, you know. None of us go on for ever."

Tania didn't know how to reply. The thought of having to uproot herself and start all over again was bad enough – but she suspected she would have to make all the arrangements for a funeral and oversee the disposal of the house and contents. She had begun to think of Ellen and Lupus as her family and couldn't bear the thought of losing them.

Ellen seemed to have drifted into a world of her own and Tania didn't dare burden her with questions.

* * *

The end came sooner than she had expected. She went in one morning to find Ellen lying still, on her back, the covers pulled to one side as if she was about to get out of bed.

Tania pulled the sheet up over her face and went downstairs to call the ambulance.

The puppy was jumping up at the back door to be let out and she shivered as she pulled it shut behind him.

How long would the ambulance be? Should she offer them a cup of tea? She felt like making a warm drink but stopped in case it seemed disrespectful.

She let Lupus in and, looking at him, felt tears come to her eyes. "Oh, Lupus, what are we going to do?" she said, hugging the little animal to her.

But Lupus wanted to go upstairs to his mistress and she would have to find a way to distract him. She picked up his ball and took it out into the garden. He retrieved it twice and the third time she threw it into the shed. When he ran in to get it she closed the door behind him.

"I'm sorry, Lupus," she said. "You've done nothing wrong. It won't be for long," and as she spoke the words she heard the doorbell ring. Lupus barked but she tried to ignore him as she went to let in the ambulance crew.

Twenty minutes later it was all over. She had some forms to fill in and a booklet to read. A doctor had been summoned and the body taken to the undertakers'.

She made a pot of tea and sat, stunned, trying to summon up the energy to get up and do something. She would have to find Ellen's personal papers. They would tell her if she had a solicitor and had made a will. Meanwhile she needed to talk to someone urgently.

She rang Ted and told him the news. "Do you want me to come round?" he asked.

"Yes, please. I've got to let Lupus out of the shed and I don't want to leave him alone in the house."

"I won't be long. Can't move as fast as I could, you know. Be brave, Tania."

"I'll try. Thanks, Ted."

Carole gave birth to a baby boy on April 4th. He weighed 8lb 2oz and had a scrap of dark hair and a very loud voice. Carole was besotted from the outset. Now she had a boy she wondered why she had ever considered a girl.

"Hallo, little Gary," she cooed as the nurse brought him to her for a feed. "Aren't you the most handsome baby that ever there was?"

She'd given Mrs Bennet the keys to her house and she'd brought baby clothes and nappies, and also cards and toys from customers in the shop.

Her pregnant friends came to admire the baby and compare notes, commenting how lucky she was to have it all over with.

Yes, but not lucky to have no-one at home to help, thought Carole. Gary was a demanding baby and she could see she wasn't going to get much sleep for a while.

When she phoned her father to tell him he had a grandson she was amazed at how positive his reaction was.

"You've changed, Dad," she said after she had accepted his effusive congratulations.

"I know. I think moving down here was the best thing I've ever done. Would you like me to come up sometime. I haven't booked any leave yet. I'll have to fit in with the old hands."

"Not yet. Give us time to get used to one another. I'll be glad to bring him down to see you in a few months. You've got room for us, haven't you?"

"Sure. I'll soon fix you up. Come before it gets cold and we can take Gary to see the sea."

"Thanks, Dad. Everything else OK?" She didn't like to mention her mother.

"So,so. It's early days – but I'm getting there."

What did that mean? she wondered. Had he given up the search? Would he rather not succeed? The answers would have to wait until she saw him again.

Tania and Ted found Ellen's papers filed neatly away in her bureau. All the bills until the last few weeks were arranged in date order and the doctor, dentist and solicitor all listed.

"Mr Trentham!" exclaimed Tania, "That must be who drove the black car. She said she'd spoken to him recently."

"He'll have her will," said Ted. "You'll soon find out what is happening with the house."

When she did find out she could hardly believe it. Ellen had left everything to her – the house, the contents and the money she had in the bank. There were no other beneficiaries and no instructions except that Tania had to look after Lupus until he died.

"Wow," she said, relating her discovery to Fiona. "I don't deserve it. What possessed her?"

"You do deserve it," said Fiona, "But you don't have to live there. You could sell it. It needs a lot of maintenance and you could look after Lupus anywhere."

"I don't think that's what she meant," said Tania, thoughtfully. "All those clothes..."

"They could be quite valuable."

"I know. That's what I was thinking."

"Well, don't decide in a hurry."

"We need to contact everyone in her address book and tell the folk at the theatre. They might want to come to the funeral. She wanted a woodland burial. I didn't even know there was anywhere near that did that. Mr Trentham said she was sure her spirit would fly up to join her grandmother – but otherwise she was perfectly rational. Poor Ellen."

"Look. You did your best for her. You made her happy. Let's just put on a good show for her. I'll help."

"Thanks Fiona. I don't know what I'd do without you two."

In the event very few turned up for the burial. It was a sunny day and Tania had done everything Ellen requested. The setting was magical – very fitting for the granddaughter of a witch, she thought. Only a handful of people returned to the house for the wake.

"I think they're just curious about the house," whispered Fiona to Tania as they made tea in the kitchen.

"That tall man with the deep voice looks familiar," said Tania.

"I think he used to run the theatre. There's no-one else I recognise except the doctor."

"He didn't stay long. It feels odd without a vicar."

"Churches and witches don't mix," Fiona giggled.

"Shsh, someone will hear you." But Tania couldn't help smiling.

Tony was fishing from the pier when he saw the woman he believed was his wife again. She was with a small black dog, clambering up over the pebbles from the sandy part of the beach. When they reached the prom she put the dog on a lead.

He didn't want to abandon his tackle but he packed it up as swiftly as he could and then hurried in the same direction as his quarry. She turned inland and into a park where she set the dog free and threw a ball for it.

"Good boy, Lupus," he heard her say and he was convinced he had at last found Barbara.

Yet he couldn't approach her. He felt paralysed with indecision. Did he want to find his wife – or would that ruin the new life he had made for himself?

She looked content and he felt a stirring of the old rage inside him She had no right to be be so happy after abandoning him. The least he could do was watch and see where she was living. Then, if there was a new man involved, he would find a way to get rid of him. He had plenty of friends, now, who would be happy to help send such an interloper packing. He'd quite relish the chance to beat the living daylights out of anyone who had taken something that belonged to him.

A few minutes later she called the dog and led him out of the park and across the road to a tall terraced house. Mounting the steps she put her key in the lock, opened the door, and went inside.

Tony waited for a while – looking up and down the road for a sign that anyone else lived there. A van was parked outside but it belonged to a window cleaner who soon drove it away.

Tony noted the house number, twenty four, and walked to the end of the road to read the name plate. His head felt fuzzy. He needed to go somewhere quiet and try to decide what to do next. One of the shops had an upstairs café that was often almost empty. The food wasn't great but he'd have a coffee and a muffin and think through his options. He'd need to stake out the place at different times of day. At least his shifts would allow him to do that – but maybe if he came back at the weekend that wouldn't be necessary. Or should he just knock on the door and see what happened?

He'd do nothing until he'd had a night's sleep, he decided. It was too much of a problem, and one he could have done without.

Tania had accepted that she was the new owner of 24 Cavendish Road. She looked around the lounge and spoke out loud, "Now we'll have to get up to date. First thing we'll have a TV in here. Then we'll start redecorating." It would be an enormous task but Ellen had left a sizeable amount of money and Tania was determined to spend it on the house.

I'll give myself a year, she thought – then I'll see if I can go back to work. I may even take up hairdressing again. Thank you, Ellen, you have given me a future.

There was a sharp rap on the front door and she went

to open it.

Tony stood on the step. He looked angry and ready to push past her.

Tania squealed and turned, almost tripping over Lupus, who barked and jumped up at her husband. Taking advantage of his actions she raced down the hall, into the kitchen and out through the back door. She could hear curses and thumps behind her but she dared not look back. It was as if the man in her dream had found her – and he looked ready to murder her and bury her in the garden!

Almost blinded by fear she ran to the back fence – climbed onto the stacked wooden pallets and bricks she had used to block the hole and scrambled over.

She looked back, then, and saw Tony thundering after her, shouting something, but she could not make it out. She heard, "Stop," and "Talk" but she did not want to do either.

He was climbing the fence behind her now and she pushed her way through the bushes. There was nowhere to hide. She ran on and found herself on the railway line.

There was a loud hoot and she saw a train speeding towards her. Could she cross the line before it came or should she go back? She froze, undecided, and as the train whistled by her with inches to spare, she felt Tony pulling her back towards him.

She sat, crying, on the verge.

He'd found her and nearly got her killed. Was that what he wanted? She'd not escaped after all.

Tony was putting something round her shoulders. "I thought you'd had it," he said a last and bent down to pull her to her feet. Then, to her surprise, he folded her in his arms and hugged her tightly.

"Tony?" she said, "Is it really you?"

"Of course. Let's go back. There's so much to tell you."

Tell me? thought Tania, When did you ever tell me anything? But she let herself be helped back over the fence and didn't even complain when she caught her skirt on the wire.

They sat across from each other at the kitchen table. Tony seemed stunned by what had happened.

He's just the same, thought Tania. He can't say what he's thinking.

"Shall I make a pot of tea?" she said, to break the silence.

Tony seemed to come out of his trance and look around. "How did you get here?" he asked.

Tania spoke with her back to him. "I was friends with the owner. She gave me somewhere to live. Why are you here?"

"I started looking for you. Then things changed. I sold the house."

"You did that already?" Tania was astonished that he had been so well organised. It was years since he had instigated any action.

"Yes. I've got a park home."

"Near here?"

"Yes, between here and Brighton - and I've got a job."

A job? After all the months of moping around moaning that retirement didn't suit him, but doing nothing about it? "Are you happy?" she asked.

"I thought I was – until I saw you. I wanted to punish you – but then – holding you." His words tailed off.

"I'm sorry." She turned to face him, hoping he would respond.

"It's funny – oh dammit – I forgot – you're a grand-mother!"

"What?"

"Carole. She's had a baby boy. She'll be so glad I found you."

Tania gasped in surprise. The shock made it hard to breathe. Carole, her daughter, not married, yet with a child. All this had happened while she was trying to carve out a new life for herself.

"I must ring her," she said at last. "When did it happen?"

"Last week. We could go and see them together."

"Oh yes – play happy families – after all we've been through," she laughed bitterly.

"OK, you go." he snapped. "I'll give you her address. If your life is so great without me I'll leave you alone. You're still the selfish bitch I thought you were." His face flushed with rage.

"Don't, Tony. It's too soon. Give me your number. I need time to take all this in," and she suddenly felt overwhelmed and burst into tears.

"God – I hate crying women," said Tony, but his voice had softened. "If you're OK I'll let myself out." He reached into his pocket, tore a page from a diary and scribbled in it. Then, leaving the page on the table, he left.

Tania almost sleepwalked into the lounge. She'd had such plans for this house. She was going to turn it into a home first and then maybe find a use for the large room on the first floor.

Now she was beginning to feel her Tania persona slipping away. She was becoming Barbara again, Barbara, who put up with a thankless husband because of promises made years ago, promises that had led to her only child, Carole, the daughter she had shut out of her new life.

She looked down at the paper in her hand. The phone number Tony had written was an unfamiliar one. Did she have the courage to ring it? Would Carole ever forgive her? All Tania's confidence had deserted her. She was Barbara once again and all she dared do was send her daughter a text.

She stared at the message screen and began to type : *I have seen your father. He told me your news. Congratulations. Can I visit? Mum.* It was enough. Carole's phone would give her a number for a reply. Tania pressed to send and then sat holding the phone in her hand. Her arm would not keep still. It was shaking with trepidation. She put the phone on the coffee table and tried to still her nerves. When nothing happened after a few minutes she began to breathe more easily but was shocked into activity when the text alarm sounded.

I'll ring you later. Carole. It wasn't much, but it was a reply. Tania began to wish that Tony hadn't left so abruptly. What could she tell Carole about their meeting – that Tony had maybe saved her life? No – that was too dramatic. Besides, if he hadn't been chasing her she wouldn't have been on the railway line.

He'd seemed different, somehow – more 'with it' as if he was involved with the world, not shut away from it.

He'd said he had a job, hadn't he? That might make all the difference. He must have tried very hard to find her. Should she be grateful or afraid?

Whatever was going to happen between her and her husband the most important thing to do now was to mend fences with her daughter. There was nothing to hold her back. She could go as soon as she was invited.

She paced the house waiting for a call. When nothing came she sorted through her clothes and packed anyway. While she was packing she realised she needed to take a present – something for the baby – but what? Making sure her phone was fully charged she ran out of the house to the main shopping area and into the first baby shop she saw.

Racks and racks of clothes, all with ages and sizes. She didn't know the size! She only knew it was a boy. She hesitated over a blue fluffy rabbit. She picked up some dungarees with a train on the front. No – he wasn't ready for that yet. She settled on a red babygro and a token so that Carole could choose for herself – and bought the rabbit anyway because she liked it.

By the time she got home, breathless but satisfied, she was beginning to worry that something might be wrong. Maybe the baby was ill – maybe Carole hated her -perhaps there had been an accident?

She made a sandwich but couldn't settle and by the time seven o'clock came she was about to risk calling her daughter again but Carole pre-empted her.

"Carole?" she said.

"Hi Mum. Am I glad you called. I was really cheesed off with not knowing where you were. I wanted you here, mum. I didn't realise how much I missed you."

"Please say you forgive me, darling. You know what your father was like. I just couldn't stand it any longer. I'm sorry I lost touch with you but your phone was cut off. I thought you hated me."

"I wish I could have been there before you left. I might have helped – but he's not like that any more. I don't know what's happened but he's changed."

"More than I have, I expect. I tried to be different but it didn't work. I so much wanted a new life but now I don't know what to do."

"Come up and stay a while, Mum – or have you a job you can't leave?"

"No – my job's finished. I'm a free agent. I'd love to come up. What have you called the baby?"

"Gary. Gary Jason Sharp. His father was married. He didn't want to know, Mum. Hell – I mustn't cry."

Tania choked back her own tears. Did she really deserve this? Maybe Tony had been right and she had been utterly selfish leaving him and their daughter. What if he had never found her and she'd never known she had a granddaughter? Why hadn't she tried harder to keep in touch with Carole? She had gone through so much and not felt able to tell her own mother.

"Give me your full address. I'll get the train up at the weekend. I take it you've moved out of the flat? Is that why I couldn't reach you?"

"Yes, I'm in Bishop. It's a sweet little house. You'd like it here, Mum. Just hearing your voice makes me feel better."

There was a high pitched wail in the background. Carole laughed. "Well, I did until his majesty wanted feeding. Keep in touch, Mum -and don't worry."

Fancy her telling me not to worry, thought Tania – but she wasn't Tania any more, was she? She was Barbara Sharp and before she went north she would have to see Mr Trentham the solicitor and explain. If it meant she didn't get the house she would feel, in a way, that she deserved to lose it – as a punishment for running away.

Twelve

Carole wanted to be angry with her mother but it was impossible. She was so excited about seeing her again and showing the house, and her grandson – having time to sit and chat – two women together. She wanted to know all about her own first few weeks and how her mother managed. She wanted to show her the area, prove how well she was coping and find out what Barbara had been doing in the months they were apart.

Most of all, she wanted to share – share the little moments of joy and surprise when Gary smiled or waved his feet in the air or just looked adorable when he was asleep. Carole was feeding him herself but had bottles ready in case he needed more when she wasn't around. Of course, so far, she hadn't let him out of her sight, but now she brushed a few strands of hair out of his eyes and cooed at him, "Grandma's coming to see you, little one. Isn't that fun?"

* * *

It was a fortnight of pure delight for both women and only ended when Barbara had a call from the solicitor. She needed to return and prove her identity with documentary evidence and, preferably, her husband.

"I do need to come clean with my friends down there," she told Carole. "I just hope they still want to know me."

"You won't be hard on Dad, will you? Give him a chance. He didn't understand why you ran away.

He thought you had everything you wanted. He couldn't believe you hadn't gone off with another man."

"It wasn't like that. He just wasn't interested in my life. We didn't share anything – not even the same jokes."

"I don't think he felt like laughing. He just felt useless and unwanted."

"I tried to get him to go out or find a hobby but he wouldn't."

"He didn't feel he was providing any money. It's different now he's earning. He's got his self esteem back."

"I suppose I wasn't very sympathetic, but don't expect too much. I'm just going to take things slowly. He's come out of this quite well but it may not last."

"I know – but as soon as Gary can travel I'm coming down to see him. I was going to stay with him but it might be better if I stay at yours."

"If I'm still there – of course – there's loads of room. I'd love to have you both."

"If he agrees that will show you how much he's changed."

"Let's just wait and see."

It was August before the legal details were finalised and 24 Cavendish Road became Barbara's.

Ted and Fiona had at first been shocked and surprised when she told them her real name and when they met Tony they found it difficult to understand why she had left him.

Barbara had bought new furniture for the lounge and invited all her friends to a house party. Pat from pilates class, Gloria and John from Downsview and the doctor and his wife were invited. She asked Tony if he wanted to bring anyone but he declined. "I'll put in an appearance later on," he said, "But it's a bit embarrassing. I don't want to be on show."

"You dress differently, now, Tony, don't you? You really have changed."

"Do you like it?"

"Of course. It's casual, but up to date. Did you shop by yourself?"

Tony laughed. "What if I didn't? Would you be jealous?"

His wife hesitated. "Maybe – but I wouldn't be surprised if you had found a girl friend."

Tony looked at her archly. "Is that a compliment?"

"Don't let it go to your head - but it's nice to be able to talk like this, isn't it?"

"Next thing, you'll be inviting yourself round to my place."

"Don't rush me. I'm just getting used to having a house of my own."

"Will you sell it?"

"I'm not sure. It depends on a lot of things. I've been very lucky."

"From what the solicitor said you worked hard."

"It was very strange – but now I've got my old name back I can find a new job."

"Yes, and I must get back, or I'll be late for mine. See you at the bus stop sometime," and he strolled away as if he didn't have a care in the world.

I wish he'd kissed me goodbye, thought Barbara. She hadn't realised how much she missed being close to a man.

Once she'd made the announcement about her name change, with the barest of details about her separation, her visitors relaxed and enjoyed the party. By the time Tony arrived, the others were full of good food and wine, music was playing and Barbara was content. She held his arm while she introduced him to everyone and Ted soon got chatting to him about the best places for fishing.

Fiona was sitting stroking Lupus and Barbara sat next to her.

"It's going to be funny calling you Barbara," she said, "Tania suits you better."

"You can still call me Tania if you like. Pretend it's a nickname – but life will be a lot easier if I go back to my married name."

"Your husband seems OK."

"He does, doesn't he? Perhaps he just needed a shake up. I get the feeling he's trying very hard to make a good impression. He won't have controlled his bad temper completely but he's certainly started to take more care of himself. He never used to go shopping. He said if he had clothes that fitted he didn't need new ones. Some of the things he had were thirty or more years old."

"He hasn't put weight on, then?"

"If he has -the clothes stretched. I suppose it was partly my fault. I just let him vegetate."

"What did you do with your time?"

"I was a hairdresser."

"Will you go back to it?"

"I'm not sure. Having this big house has given me some ideas."

"Really? Do tell."

"When I'm ready. A lot of it depends on Carole. She's bringing the baby for a week in September."

"I hope the weather stays fine."

"So do I. I want to show her the area."

"Tony seems to like being by the sea."

"I can't see him as a fisherman."

"Have you seen his home yet?"

"No. I'm not sure I want to. When we were together he was always happier in a room by himself."

"Oh, Tania. I am sorry. I hoped you could get back together."

"It's a nice thought – but he's almost a different man. I need to get used to him again."

"He looks at you as if he likes you."

"Well, he's not used to me as a blonde. We've both changed. Nothing would be the same."

Tony looked round his little home. He'd got everything he wanted there, in one place, everything except a woman in his life.

Seeing Barbara again had confused him. He almost resented the fact that she had intruded into his new life – reminding him of the man he used to be.

It couldn't have been all his fault, could it? Somehow she must have allowed him to drift into being the miserable old git he now felt he had been.

He still felt grumpy occasionally -life couldn't be easy all the time – but he wasn't losing his temper as often as he had when he was with her. She had seemed to trigger something in him that made him hit out. She made him doubt himself, and she talked too much.

No, he decided, he didn't want to go back to living with his wife. All the same, she did look fit and she'd felt right when she was in his arms. It would be simpler to get cozy with her than with a new woman. He'd have to be crafty – maybe send her some flowers. He couldn't remember the last time he'd done that. Not yet, though,he still had to cope with the visit from Carole and the baby.

Once alone in 24 Cavendish Road Barbara paced the floor trying to decide what to do with the house.

She'd hoped to be able to use the first floor as a child-minding area – but once she looked into the rules and regulations, with the extra toilet facilities and the need to be on the ground floor, she realised it was not feasible.

"What would you really like?" asked Fiona one day as they sat in the garden with the dogs playing round them.

"I'd like Carole to come down and live with me," answered Barbara. "I would let her have the whole first floor. There would be a bedroom for her, an office and a really big room for Gary – along with the bathroom and toilet. It would almost be a self contained flat, but we'd have to share the kitchen."

"What do you think she'd say to that?"

"Probably no. She's got a sweet little house up there, all her own, and she likes the area."

"You don't think she'd give that up to get a permanent babysitter?"

"I didn't think of that. Of course, she could go back to work."

"You could still do part time, back in the hairdressers."

"I'd need to, but not until Gary started at nursery. I wonder if it's worth suggesting?"

"Try it. She can only say no."

So Barbara phoned her daughter and made the suggestion.

Carole was non committal. "Wait until I come down, Mum. We'll discuss it then," she said and Barbara had to be satisfied with that.

She went back to the hairdressers she had been using and told the owner she was looking for work.

"You can hire a chair – for two days a week to start with – and see how it goes," she said.

"Thanks – and I think I might try the college to see if I can get a refresher course."

On Barbara's birthday a large bunch of flowers was delivered to the house, along with an invitation to dinner at a local restaurant. It was from Tony and Barbara was torn between pleasure that he had remembered and anger that he had left it so late.

Luckily she had planned a lunch with Ted and Fiona rather than dinner as Ted didn't like to eat late in the evening – but she still raged at them. "I don't know how much to eat! He said he'd pick me up at 6.30. He's not told me what to wear! It's just too disorganised."

"Don't be too hard on him. Give him a chance," said Fiona. "You do still have feelings for him, don't you?"

"Oh yes, feelings of irritation and annoyance! My life was quite all right before he came blundering back into it. Now I'm in a complete muddle."

"You didn't tell him to go away."

"No – perhaps I should have done – but that wouldn't be fair on Carole. Trust him to spoil my birthday!"

When Tony turned up at 6.30 wearing a suit, Barbara was glad she had dressed smartly. She was wearing a cream trouser suit with a chocolate blouse. Trousers, she felt, warned him there would be no fraternising after the meal.

Fiona and Ted had given her some new gold earrings shaped like shells and she felt ready for anything her husband could say to her.

They drove out of town in silence. Tony kept sneaking sideways glances at her as if he couldn't quite believe she was there.

The restaurant was part of a large chain – but in a romantic looking beamed barn with chairs and tables in nooks and crannies. The atmosphere was warm and friendly and the menu extensive.

"What would you like to drink?" asked Tony at last.

"I don't know. I'll have a pineapple juice for now and then choose something that goes with what I'm eating."

Tony ordered a cider and they were escorted to a corner table.

"How do you manage, making your own meals?" Barbara asked.

"I don't do many. I've got good at breakfast – but the rest of the time I get pies or fish and chips or eat out. Great thing about living down here there's plenty of places to eat."

"Do you eat the fish you catch?"

"Sometimes, or I give it to Marge. She and Glen live in Brighton. They looked after me after my accident."

"You had an accident?"

"Yes, that's why I've got a different car. Only a bump – but I was in hospital for a bit."

"I'm sorry, Tony. I didn't know."

"There's a lot you didn't know, isn't there?" His voice grew harder, but he seemed to check himself. "Don't lets get into that. Anything there you fancy?" and he gestured at the menu.

Barbara studied it as thoroughly as she could but the words seemed to blur. Feelings of guilt were making it hard to concentrate. Had her departure made Tony drive more carelessly? She couldn't imagine him having an accident. He was always so trustworthy behind the wheel. He wouldn't drink more than the cider he had ordered and the old Tony would have refused to buy a single glass of wine. She fancied salmon – but it was one of the most expensive items on the menu. How much could he afford and what would he consider extravagant? "Could I have a glass of the house white wine, please?" she ventured.

"It's a birthday treat," he said, as if he was reading her mind. "Have what you like."

"What are you having?"

"Steak and kidney pie."

"I'll have the scampi. Ellen would never have it in the house."

"She was a bit of an odd ball, then, was she? How did you get tied up with her?"

Barbara told him,then – about her desire to be someone different and how she realised she could never get regular employment with a new name. She found herself telling him about the dogs and the stage room and how Ellen's fantasies developed into an illness that resulted in her death.

"And she left you the house?"

"Yes – and I'm not sure what to do with it. I suppose I should either sell it or get lodgers."

The conversation was halted by the arrival of their meal and Barbara waited until they had chosen and enjoyed their desserts, miniature sussex puddings, before she asked him more about himself.

He told her about his new job driving buses and asked her if she would like to see his new home.

"Another day, perhaps," Barbara demurred. "I think I'm too tired to appreciate it now."

"Guess it does look better in daylight," said Tony, "Come on Saturday, about eleven."

"That would be lovely, Tony. Thanks for a special evening."

"We don't do so bad, do we?"

"In small doses," she laughed.

"Right – back to the mansion it is. Happy Birthday, love."

And it has been, thought Barbara as she got ready for bed that night. Tony had left her with a chaste kiss on the cheek and she had sat daydreaming in the kitchen until she felt she had to get some sleep.

But sleep did not come easily. She had so many decisions to make. She needed to modernise the house and get it ready for Carole's visit. She would not be rushed by her husband. She might not be called Tania any more but she still cherished her independence.

Thirteen

Carole was sobbing. "I don't know what you want, now," she said to the baby. "I've fed you and changed you. You are warm enough and comfortable enough and I'm so tired. Why don't you let me sleep!"

She picked up the wailing baby and held him over her shoulder, gently rocking from one foot to the other. His cries turned to hiccups and he dribbled down her back – but he was no longer yelling. She walked him up and down and put her face next to his. "You smell all milky," she said softly, "I know what we'll do - we'll put some music on."

Tubular bells rang through the little house and the baby's eyes began to close. Carole transferred him to her lap and then when he didn't wake, laid him in his cot and stroked his face gently. He blew a bubble but stayed asleep.

"Now it's my turn," she said and, slipping off her shoes, climbed into the bed and covered herself with the duvet.

She was woken by the usual hungry grizzle but she felt better and was happy to feed him. Looking round her bedroom she realised how she had come to love this house, yet her mother's suggestion had made her think. If she stayed up north she would have to find childcare for Gary when she went back to work – but if she accepted her mother's offer she would have both a home and someone to care for him while she worked.

She wouldn't have to sell the house. She was sure she could let it – perhaps to a lecturer at Durham University. It would be an investment for the future, and if staying with her mother didn't work out she could come back, couldn't she?

She would decide when she saw the place. If she liked it she would move. Gary would enjoy being near the seaside and he wouldn't be far from his granddad. He would need a male role model and, although Tony wasn't perfect, he was the only family to hand and he seemed ready to give attention to his grandchild. It might even do her father some good.

Barbara surveyed the large room with pride – new soft flooring, a cot, bright yellow walls with a frieze of little trains, a blue teddy bear and a baby monitor. A cupboard with plenty of nappies. What else would they need? A basket chair for nursing and a sofa bed so that Carole could choose whether to sleep in the same room as her son or in her own bedroom next door.

Barbara had discovered a connecting door from the baby's room to Ellen's bedroom. It had been hidden by the stage set but would now prove most convenient.

The little dressing room had been stripped of most of its cupboards and the mirror moved into the bedroom. In its place was a computer desk and a chair. Fiona had introduced her to her local friendly 'computer nerd' and he had made sure she had wi-fi connection with the new TV. She hadn't bought a computer. She would wait until Carole was down and get her advice – but if her daughter didn't move in she would take classes. She was determined to keep up with the times.

It was Saturday and Barbara had insisted she was quite capable of finding Tony's home by herself.

The bus along the coast stopped right outside the entrance and she only had to walk a few yards before she saw him outside a white caravan.

It had a sizeable lean-to on the side and a tiny plot of garden with paving stones and tubs of plants.

The front was one large bay window and the whole thing looked bright and welcoming.

"Come in, come in," said Tony. "I'll get you a coffee. Do you want a tour or just a sit down in the lounge?"

"I think in here would be lovely," Barbara called out as she entered the roomy stylish sitting room.

"There's a nest of tables in the corner," responded Tony. "I won't be a tick."

Barbara chose a leather armchair and looked around her. The place was very neat and tidy – but not minimalistic. She pulled out a table as Tony brought in a tray.

"Coffee and jaffa cakes OK?" he asked.

"Lovely, Tony. This is very smart."

"Not all new, but I like it. Not too near the other

vans, either."

"I see you've got a garden."

"Well, a patio. Best thing is the porch – but I'll show you round later. How's Carole?"

"Coming next month – I've got the flat ready. I'm going to ask if she'd like to live there."

"What a good idea. She was coming here, until I found you. Then, of course, it was back to her mother's."

"I'm sorry, Tony. Would you have had room?"

"Oh yes. There's two decent sized bedrooms." He paused.

I don't know what to say next, thought Barbara. I shouldn't have come. She had to change the subject. "When do you go fishing?"

"When the tide's right -or when Glen and the boys take a boat out. Would you like to meet them sometime?"

"Don't rush me, Tony."

"Sorry."

They drank their coffee in silence and when Tony took out the mugs Barbara followed him into the kitchen. "This is very nice."

"Yep."

"And the bathroom?"

"Just along there. I'll show you."

He was waiting for her when she had washed her hands and he pushed open the door of the end room. "The master bedroom," he announced and stood back to let her see.

She did not enter. She just nodded and backed away.

"And the spare room is here," he said, and opened the final door.

It was a pretty, square room with a single bed with a floral bedspread.

"There's room for a cot. I was going to get a travel one."

"I'm sorry. I expect they would have loved staying here."

"No. They're better off with you. I'm not too good with babies," he smiled. "How about a walk on the beach?"

"I'd like that – and you can show me your fishing gear."

They seemed to relax, then, and the tension in the air vanished. Barbara was glad she had worn flat shoes. There was no way she could traipse over the cobbles in heels.

He seems very settled, she thought. Even more than she was – and she put out her hand to hold his as they crossed the road.

She was rewarded with a beaming smile. Amazing, she thought, She'd forgotten how handsome he looked when he was happy.

They ate fish and chips at a café on the beach and Barbara felt reluctant to go home – but once back inside the caravan she felt awkward again and asked Tony if he could drive her back.

"I didn't check the bus times," she said, "What a fool."

"It's only a ten minute run," said Tony, "Save you the bus fare."

She'd given the impression that she had an appointment. She hadn't – but she needed to be by herself. 'Stop the World – I want to get off!' she thought, as she waved him away and entered number 24.

* * *

Tony was in a turmoil. He'd had a date with his wife and shown her his new home. He'd spent the afternoon with her and it had seemed so natural. It was like going back twenty years.

The problem was, he still fancied her – even with short, blonde hair. He'd had to stop himself pulling her into the bedroom and acting like her husband... He was her husband, after all! Yet he knew it would spoil everything. It would be hard to take things at her pace but he had hopes. There was no-one who understood him as well as she did. He would have to be patient. Tomorrow he would see his friends. They would want to know how he was managing. How much would he tell them? What he needed was an excuse to bring her to some kind of social occasion. He poured himself a rum and coke and turned on the TV. Life was getting better by the second!

"I'm sorry, Tony. I'm busy that day," said Barbara when he invited her to a barbecue in Brighton.

She wasn't. She was lying – but she didn't feel ready to be considered his partner again. They would be treated as 'an item' and that was not what she wanted. In fact, she wished she hadn't abandoned her alternative identity so readily.

She had found a job, but being Barbara Sharp made her feel tethered again.

Tony sounded disappointed and she could sense the suppressed anger in his voice. Still, at least it was suppressed. She still wasn't sure he was a changed man.

She was obliged to ask him to pick Carole and Gary up from the station and he was civil enough when they were all together but the carefree feeling that she had experienced on Saturday had evaporated and they both let Carole carry the conversation over dinner.

Tony left before Gary went to bed and Carole and Barbara sat together in the lounge staring at one another like strangers. Then Carole burst out laughing. "What a difference, Mum."

"Difference, how?"

"With you, this house, Dad, everything. Life's completely odd, unexpected. What made you do it, Mum?"

"What? Run away? I told you. Your father made my life unbearable."

"But he's not like that any more."

"I know and I can't get used to it."

"When you left it shook him up."

"He needed it."

"You were cruel, Mum."

"Cruel to be kind."

"You didn't mean to be kind, though, did you? You just wanted a different life."

"Yes – but when I found it, it wasn't what I expected. The poor old lady who lived here was ill and I had to nurse her."

"But she left you the house."

"I still need to work to maintain it. It could be a burden."

"But not if I come to live here, and pay rent."

"Would you?"

"Let's see how this week goes. It's certainly an option."

*　*　*

Tony's friends all wanted to know about the reappearance of his wife.

He didn't like to talk about it. In a way he was glad she had refused to come to the barbecue.

Marge took him aside. "Tony, a word of advice. If you can, keep your mobile home on. Don't expect to move in with Barbara. There's loads of people happier living apart than in the same house. You could still be good friends."

"I'd like to be more than that, Marge."

"I know and for your sake I hope it happens."

Tony shrugged. It was still summer and girls were walking about in shorts or bikinis. What was a man to do? How long could he be patient?

By the time she was ready to go back, Carole had made up her mind. The flat in Cavendish Road was too good an opportunity to pass up.

She and her mother would bring up her son together. She could help look after the house and garden and Gary would have all the space he needed, with the sea a few hundred yards away and a dog as a playmate.

She made tentative enquiries at three local estate agents, two of whom seemed very interested.

The pay was better than she had been getting up north.

All she had to do now was to find a tenant for the little house. She would miss it, but it would still be hers.

December saw the family settling into a routine.

Tony filled the time when he was not at work with

fishing, darts and his friends in Brighton.

He came over to Barbara's for dinner at least once a week and dropped in during the day when he finished work early or before a shift.

Barbara was friendly but insisted she had no time to go out as she had to stay with Gary. Nevertheless she began to grow used to having him around. He took an interest in his grandson and together they laughed at the baby's antics. It was so nice having someone to enjoy life with and Barabara started to look forward to their time together. She sometimes caught him giving her a curious glance, as if he wanted to ask a question but dare not. Could they ever get back the closeness they once had?

It was Carole who went out in the evenings and it was Carole who began to mix with people outside the home.

Whereas Barbara only used the Leisure Centre for pilates, Carole went to the swimming pool and joined various activities there.

She was away from home the day Tony dropped in with a Christmas tree and a load of parcels. Together, he and Barbara dressed the tree and Barbara made them drinks and mince pies.

They sat together on the sofa, reminiscing about previous Christmases and Tony took the opportunity to give Barbara a kiss.

To his surprise she responded and they hugged fiercely before moving apart. "I still want you, you know," he whispered.

"I wondered. Would you like to try?" She blushed.

"You mean- go upstairs?"

"Yes," she laughed, "I didn't mean do it here!"

"Lead the way. You never know, you might even enjoy it."

His smile made her feel a tenderness that she hadn't felt for years. He'd been so sweet – and she'd been a misery. They were still married, after all!

Afterwards she lay with him spooned against her back. She felt lighter somehow – as if a taut wire had been loosened.

He was relaxed all right. He'd gone to sleep – but she was suppose to be babysitting Gary. A fine babysitter she was!

She didn't want to move. It felt so right having her husband next to her again – but that didn't mean she wanted it to be a permanent arrangement. It had been a treat – and that's how she wanted it to stay.

She wriggled out of the bed and got dressed. Hopefully Carole would be so enthralled with the tree she wouldn't guess what had been going on – but she would have to wake Tony before her daughter came home.

He was reluctant to leave. "Why shouldn't she know her mother and father are back together again?"

"That's not how it is."

"But you liked it."

"Of course I did – but go home and think about it. That was fine but I don't want us to go back to how we were. You're happier now and I don't want to spoil it."

"You mean, just get together sometimes?"

"Yes. I'm not going anywhere."

"I'll miss you tonight," He smiled.

"Go on, go home and gloat, you randy old thing!"

"Sexpot!"

She laughed.

"You're lovely," he said.

"And you're too smooth," and she handed him his coat.

"Oh baby, it's cold out there," he sang.

"Get away with you – and thanks."

"For the tree?"

"For everything."

She closed the door softly behind him. I was flirting with my own husband, she thought, Whatever next?

She was still standing by the door when the key turned in the lock.

"Hi, Mum. Going out?"

"No. Your father just dropped in with a tree."

"Wow – let's see." She ran into the lounge where the tree stood covered in baubles and tinsel.

"It's got lights," said Barbara. "I'll turn them on."

"We must open the curtains, "said Carole, "Let the world see them."

"Just 'till we go to bed. Did you have a good evening?"

"Yes, brilliant - and I'd like you to meet someone. I'm so lucky. I've fallen in love."

"That was quick."

"Not really. We've been seeing each other for three months. I didn't tell you before. I had to be sure he was special. He's a schoolteacher. He knows I've got a baby."

"A schoolteacher. I suppose you met him through work. Did you find him a house?"

"No. He's renting at the moment. He can't afford a house."

"Oh, Carole. He's not just after somewhere cheap to live is he?"

"Mother! Wait till you meet him. He's quiet and funny and looks like he needs feeding up. Here, I've got a photo."

She brought out her mobile phone and clicked a button.

A thin young man with long sandy hair was smiling at the camera.

"Well, bring him round at the weekend. What's his name?"

"Adrian, Adrian King."

Yes, of course, someone the old house was waiting for, thought Barbara, A. King.

* * *